MAGIC
BELOW STAIRS

MAGIC
BELOW STAIRS
~ BY ~
CAROLINE STEVERMER

DIAL BOOKS FOR YOUNG READERS
AN IMPRINT OF PENGUIN GROUP (USA) INC.

To Julia, who knows Bess
better than I do

DIAL BOOKS FOR YOUNG READERS
A division of Penguin Young Readers Group · Published by The Penguin Group

Penguin Group (USA) Inc., 375 Hudson Street, New York, NY 10014, U.S.A. · Penguin Group (Canada), 90 Eglinton Avenue East, Suite 700, Toronto, Ontario, Canada M4P 2Y3 (a division of Pearson Penguin Canada Inc.) · Penguin Books Ltd, 80 Strand, London WC2R 0RL, England · Penguin Ireland, 25 St. Stephen's Green, Dublin 2, Ireland (a division of Penguin Books Ltd) · Penguin Group (Australia), 250 Camberwell Road, Camberwell, Victoria 3124, Australia (a division of Pearson Australia Group Pty Ltd) · Penguin Books India Pvt Ltd, 11 Community Centre, Panchsheel Park, New Delhi - 110 017, India · Penguin Group (NZ), 67 Apollo Drive, Rosedale, North Shore 0632, New Zealand (a division of Pearson New Zealand Ltd) · Penguin Books (South Africa) (Pty) Ltd, 24 Sturdee Avenue, Rosebank, Johannesburg 2196, South Africa · Penguin Books Ltd, Registered Offices: 80 Strand, London WC2R 0RL, England

1 3 5 7 9 10 8 6 4 2

LIBRARY OF CONGRESS CATALOGING-IN-PUBLICATION DATA
Stevermer, Caroline.
    Magic below stairs / by Caroline Stevermer.
        p. cm.
    Summary: Ten-year-old Frederick, who is surreptitiously watched over by a brownie, is plucked from a London orphanage to be a servant to a wealthy wizard, and eventually his uncanny abilities lead him to become the wizard's apprentice.
    ISBN 978-0-8037-3467-8 (hardcover)
    [1. Magic—Fiction. 2. Orphans—Fiction. 3. Wizards—Fiction. 4. Household employees—Fiction. 5. Great Britain—History—1800–1837—Fiction.] I. Title.
    PZ7.S84856Mag 2010
    [Fic]—dc22
                            2009025100

CONTENTS

IN WHICH FREDERICK
MAKES HIMSELF USEFUL

The first time he met Billy Bly, Frederick thought he must be dreaming. Billy Bly looked like a little old man dressed all in green, and came just to Frederick's knee. He was small enough to have no difficulty retrieving the dried beans and peas that had been scattered under the cupboard and into the farthest darkest corners of the kitchen. In fact, he seemed delighted to count and sort them, his voice as deep as the hum of bees, and he worked so steadily that the rattle of them in the buckets made a soothing sound like raindrops falling.

The peas and beans had been scattered everywhere as punishment. That winter night Mr. Makepeace—the director of the orphanage where Frederick had lived for as long as he could remember—had discovered Frederick in the kitchen breaking the rules. Frederick had been helping Vardle the cook peel potatoes, in return for all the peelings he could eat. If the peelings were clean enough, Frederick could eat a surprising number of them, and he had.

But no orphan was allowed in the kitchen. That was one of the many rules. Mr. Makepeace never liked to see the orphans getting anything extra to eat, for he believed it only made them more likely to be disobedient. Vardle the cook ignored lots of Mr. Makepeace's rules, especially when he wanted help in the kitchen. Vardle liked Frederick.

Mr. Makepeace disliked orphans in general. Ever since the day Frederick, shoved by one of the bigger orphans, had fallen downstairs and landed on Mr. Makepeace's hat, which was never the same again, Mr. Makepeace had disliked Frederick in particular. That was one reason Vardle the cook liked Frederick.

Mr. Makepeace had shouted at Frederick and sworn at Vardle. Then he emptied a five-pound bag of beans and a three-pound bag of peas right in the middle of the kitchen floor. It was like scattering gravel. Peas and beans went everywhere.

"Pick those up," Mr. Makepeace ordered Frederick. "I want them cleaned and sorted and the floor fresh-scrubbed by morning, or it's a day locked inside the still room for you. Use those buckets there. No tricks, like sweeping them up and rinsing them off. Pick them up with your dirty hands, you dreadful boy."

To the cook, Mr. Makepeace snarled, "He is to have no help from you, Vardle. Understand?" He went on and on. Frederick got to work while Mr. Makepeace made his threats.

If Vardle the cook did anything further that Mr. Makepeace could complain about, he would be sacked, out of a job. That was why Vardle hardly spoke a word to Frederick the rest of the evening, even though Frederick was on his hands and knees underfoot the whole time the cook prepared dinner and cleaned up afterward.

Frederick couldn't blame him. Vardle liked his job.

And besides, it wasn't Vardle who would spend the next day hungry in the still room if he failed to sort the peas and beans to Mr. Makepeace's satisfaction. Frederick had been shut in the still room before, and each time it happened, he hated it more.

The still room was a small damp storage area with a heavy lock on the door. It served as the orphanage prison cell, where offenders could be locked away alone for hours, nothing to do but sit still and repent their sins. Without a single window, even in daylight the room was dark as night. Beetles loved the still room. No one else did.

As Frederick worked with only raw potato peelings in his belly, dinner smelled better than usual, but he didn't dare ask Vardle for even a taste. Vardle may have

liked Frederick more than most of the orphans, but
not well enough to risk the sack.

Frederick did his best to keep his mind off the still
room beetles by counting the peas and beans he picked
up. Every time he reached one hundred, he let himself
imagine he had the keys to the still room. He pictured
Mr. Makepeace locked up in the dark, swearing with
fury as he swatted beetles away. Then it was back to
work until he'd picked up another hundred.

For hours, Frederick sorted peas and beans and beans
and peas. At last, the cooking and serving and washing
up was all done. Vardle put out the oil lamps and went
to bed, leaving Frederick only the light of the kitchen
fire to work by.

It was hopeless. Frederick rubbed at his stinging
eyes with sore fingers. He would never be finished by
morning. But if he gave up and tried to slip into the
dormitory now, one of the bigger boys would be sure
to catch him and turn him in to Mr. Makepeace. That
would only get him locked in the still room sooner.
Might as well keep at his task, Frederick judged.

One by one by one by one, Frederick picked up
beans and peas until his knees hurt and the tips of
his grimy fingers were raw. At last, weariness claimed
Frederick. He was so tired, his ears were buzzing, a soft
rustling sound. At first it made him think of beetles,
but soon it became dry leaves in the wind. Exhausted,

his task little more than half finished, he slept where he lay on the damp stone floor of the kitchen.

The sound of a deep soft voice counting had brought Frederick back to his senses. When Frederick woke—*if* he woke—there was still a bit of light from the fire. In the glow, he could just see a little old man, a *very* little man, hardly bigger than a cat, toiling away intently. The little man gathered peas and beans, counted them, sorted them, and darted back into the shadows after more.

As he worked, the little man sang very softly. *"Peas and beans, corn and rye, who can work like Billy Bly?"*

Frederick tried to make himself believe his eyes and ears, but his eyelids were too heavy and soon sleep overwhelmed him completely.

When Frederick woke the next morning, the kitchen floor looked freshly scrubbed. There beside him was a bucket of beans and a bucket of peas, and no sign of anyone in the kitchen, large or small, except Vardle. Frederick could not understand just how, but he knew he was saved from the still room. All he had to do was take credit for work he had left unfinished.

"Blow me down but you're a hard worker, lad." The cook put a bowl of gruel down in front of Frederick. "Get that inside you. You've made a proper job of it, no mistake. Someday when Mr. Makepeace isn't looking, I'll show you how to clean fish."

Mr. Makepeace came down to the kitchen no doubt

ready to shout and swear some more. But when he saw the floor clean and the buckets full, his eyes bulged. He ran his hands through the beans and the peas.

"Not a grain of sand," Mr. Makepeace marveled. "Not a speck of dirt." He glared at Vardle.

The cook said, "I never. He did it all by himself."

Mr. Makepeace stared at Frederick. "Who helped you?"

Frederick was an honest young fellow, but he knew it was best not to tell people like Mr. Makepeace things they would not care to know. He hesitated.

Mr. Makepeace roared at Frederick. "Who helped you?"

Frederick's ears began to buzz a little, a soft sound like dry leaves rustling. At last Frederick answered, "No one."

Mr. Makepeace poked once more at the beans, as if he couldn't believe they were real. Then, glaring so hard the whites of his eyes showed, he looked all around the room. At last, he said, "Frederick, from now on, you're the kitchen boy. Do as Vardle tells you or it will be the worse for you."

Frederick did not understand what had happened. He was just grateful to be free of the still room and its beetles. But from that day on, Mr. Makepeace stayed well away from the kitchen, and Frederick stayed well away from Mr. Makepeace.

"I do like a quiet life," Vardle said one day. "I reckon I have you to thank for it, lad. Now Mr. Makepeace has taken such a misliking to the very sight of you, he isn't down here as often, so there's far less fuss and botheration."

This encouraged Frederick to ask, "Mr. Vardle, have you ever heard of anyone who saw little men dressed all in green?"

Vardle laughed. "Little men dressed all in green? Do you mean leprechauns? They see them all the time in Ireland, so they say."

"Not in Ireland. Here."

"I myself never saw or heard of such a thing, not even in the Royal Navy." Vardle looked Frederick over carefully. "If I were you, I wouldn't mention little men, green or any other color. Keep a silent tongue in a wise head, young Frederick. That's good advice for anyone."

Frederick knew better than to ask any of the other orphans about the little man. He didn't fancy being pushed down the stairs again. He kept his mouth shut, his thoughts to himself, and his eyes and ears wide open.

Day by day, Frederick worked in the kitchen. Soon the floor no longer seemed so damp and dirty. Indeed, the whole place seemed cleaner and tidier, if no warmer. Winter was slow to take its leave that year, and spring even slower to come. Frederick was glad of the kitchen scraps he earned and happy to spend most of his time away from the other orphans.

In the kitchen, Vardle taught Frederick his duties.

"The first thing to know about cleaning fish," he told Frederick, "is that you need a sharp knife." Fish by fish, he showed Frederick the best way to remove the innards and scales. He showed Frederick which fish were worth the trouble of taking the bones out and which were not. He even showed Frederick how to make a fish stew tasty enough that the orphans would eat it every Friday without much complaint.

Frederick picked things up fast. The second thing he learned about cleaning fish was that Vardle wasn't nearly as careful to remove bones, scales, and innards as he could have been, probably because Vardle wouldn't be among those eating the result. The cook made his own meals separately out of the best of the orphanage supplies left after Mr. Makepeace had had his share.

When Frederick begged him to, Vardle, who had learned to read in the Royal Navy, used a bit of chalk on the kitchen floor to show Frederick numbers and letters of the alphabet and how to read and write them. After a few months, Frederick could read the labels on crates and sacks of provisions as well as Vardle could.

One day when Frederick was helping, he said, "It

helps you that I know the right way to clean fish, doesn't it, Mr. Vardle, sir?"

"That it does, lad," said Vardle. "The first thing you need is a sharp knife."

"Yes, Mr. Vardle, sir." Frederick did not mention that Vardle had told him so at least a dozen times. "It would be useful if I could sharpen the knives for you, wouldn't it?"

"It might be." Vardle added fresh stains to the dirty apron he wore as he scratched his round belly. "You want something, or you wouldn't be calling me *Mr. Vardle, sir.* Spit it out, lad."

"I want to learn how to sharpen a kitchen knife, that's all. Couldn't you teach me?" Frederick did his best to look trustworthy.

Vardle frowned. "The first thing to know about sharpening a knife is that you can cripple yourself if you aren't careful."

"I could have guessed that," said Frederick. "What's the second thing?"

"Oh, all right then. Since you've taken a notion to learn, the good Lord above knows why, I'll show you. Take a close look at the edge, see what you'll be working with." The cook brought out his sharpening stone. "Put your stone like this. Hold the knife so. Now, bring it toward you. What did I tell you about crippling yourself? Slower, lad."

Step by step, Vardle taught Frederick the best way to sharpen knives. After that, in addition to his usual chores, Frederick sharpened all the kitchen knives regularly.

One day Vardle told Frederick he had never worked anyplace where knives were better cared for. "You've the knack of it, no question, and lucky it is you do, for a dull knife is the most dangerous thing in any kitchen. A sharp knife cuts what you want it to cut. A dull knife cuts only what it pleases."

"The most dangerous thing in this kitchen is Mr. Makepeace," said Frederick. "But he doesn't come down so often these days. Why doesn't he?"

"Why do you think?" Vardle countered.

Mr. Makepeace had kept well away from him ever since the night of the bean and pea punishment, and Frederick wondered if Mr. Makepeace suspected something about the little man in green. It hardly seemed wise to bring that up to Vardle. So he said, "Maybe we've just been lucky."

"Lucky?" Vardle laughed heartily at the idea. "Good luck is more than half hard work. Mr. Makepeace knows things are shipshape down here, so he doesn't need to spare the effort."

One day when he was scrubbing beets for dinner, Frederick said, "Mr. Vardle, sir—"

"Here it comes," said Vardle. "Less of the best lamp oil, if you please."

"Lamp oil?" Frederick had no idea what Vardle was talking about.

"I mean less of the *Mr.-Vardle-sir*. Can tell you were raised in an orphanage. You have no more idea how to polish the brass than a sparrow would. Less, if anything."

"Brass?" Frederick wondered if Vardle had lost his wits. "I'm scrubbing the beets, not the brass."

"You only talk respectful—polish the brass, that is, or use the lamp oil—when you want me to teach you something." Puffing with effort, Vardle brought over another large bag of beets. "What is it this time?"

Frederick watched Vardle tear open the burlap bag with his big red hands. "I was only going to say you must know lots of useful things. When I grow up and join the Royal Navy, I will need to know lots of useful things myself. But since you mentioned it, what else can you teach me?"

"I already taught you all the things I know best: cleaning fish, sharpening knives, and reading the alphabet. I don't rightly know what else I know." Vardle presented Frederick with the open bag. "Scrub these like a good fellow while I think it over."

It took Vardle a long time to think of an answer to Frederick's question. When every beet was scrubbed and ready for the pot, he told Frederick, "I know how to tie knots. I could teach you that. Not that you've any use for such knowledge. You're far too young to join the Royal Navy."

"I'm getting older every day," said Frederick. "Teach me to tie knots."

Vardle found a bit of kitchen twine and held it out with each end pinched between thick finger and thicker thumb. "All right. I'll start with something simple. This is a bowline. First you make a bit of a loop, like this. Then this end goes into the loop like this, right over left, see? Pay close attention now."

One at a time, with many mistakes, Frederick learned to tie every single knot Vardle knew, from a bowline to a barrel hitch. He worked so hard, he nearly forgot about Billy Bly, the little man dressed all in green. By the end of the winter, he had mastered every knot. Frederick could tie two ropes together so they would not come apart until the moment he wished them to. He could shorten a rope without cutting it, or splice a broken rope so it was as strong as it had ever been. In the kitchen there wasn't much call for tying knots, but Frederick knew the knowledge he mastered now would help him in the Royal Navy later. In the Royal Navy, or in whatever else awaited him in life. The world outside the orphanage was enormous, and he was getting older every day.

IN WHICH FREDERICK
FINDS PAID EMPLOYMENT

When Frederick was very nearly eleven years old, a tall, elegantly dressed man came to the orphanage from one of the great houses in the richest part of the city. He was a servant there, although he was a very superior servant indeed, and he wished to engage an orphan to fill the position of footboy. He brought a suit of livery with him, dark blue coat and white knee breeches, and he announced with great authority that the lad who fit the livery best would be engaged.

Peter and Tom, older boys too big to fit the livery, whispered behind their grimy hands about the tall, solemn-looking man. "That's the man who works for the wizard," Frederick heard Peter say.

"Wizard?" Frederick couldn't help speaking aloud, he was so surprised. "He works for a wizard?"

The older boys shoved him about for a moment or

two, but it was worth it, for Tom, the smaller of the pair, answered Frederick's question. "Don't you remember? He was here about a year ago. He picked Georgie Biddle to work as bootboy in the wizard's house."

"He doesn't remember." Peter pushed Tom aside to loom over Frederick. "Where were you, under a rock?"

"Locked in the still room with his beetle friends, more likely," Tom said. "Where's Georgie now, do you think? Did the wizard grind his bones to make his bread?"

Peter lost interest in Frederick as he and Tom got into a scuffle. Frederick edged away from them, but Tom's words stayed with him.

A wizard. The orphanage was all Frederick knew. No one wanted to stay there. But would it be any better to be a wizard's servant? Would there be beetles in a wizard's house? Or would there be something even worse?

Despite his fears, Frederick noticed every orphan even close to the right size vied for the chance to escape the orphanage and find paid employment. They weren't afraid to go work for a wizard. There were a great many boys, and trying on the livery took a long time. It took so long that the solemn man had to leave before the line was finished.

"I regret that my duties call me away for now. I

shall return tomorrow morning to view the rest of the candidates," the man told Mr. Makepeace. "Is there somewhere this suit of clothes may be kept safely until then?"

"I shall put it under lock and key," said Mr. Makepeace. "No one shall touch it until you return in the morning."

Frederick didn't fancy his chances much, but when at last his turn came to try it on, late the next day, the suit of clothes fit so well, it might have been made just for him. When Mr. Makepeace was asked to provide a character reference for Frederick, he heaped so much praise on Frederick, it was embarrassing. Frederick had to keep his eyes on the floor, he was so bashful at hearing such lies told on his behalf. No doubt about it, he decided. Mr. Makepeace was willing to do anything to be rid of Frederick. He wondered why. Did it bother him that much to have Frederick helping Vardle in the kitchen?

Only Vardle showed regret when he learned that Frederick would be leaving. "I'll miss you, lad. I'll even miss the way you are forever pestering me to teach you new things. I wish you could stay, but wishing peels no onions." The cook clapped Frederick on the shoulder and added, "For all you're half the size of some of these lads, you've always done the work of two, and two clever lads at that. Most times you've done it without ever needing to be told what ought to be done. Keep that up and you'll go far in the Royal Navy. One day I'll be proud to tell my friends, there goes Frederick Lincoln. I had the teaching of him when he was only a lad, and now he's a fine young man. Won't that be a grand day?"

In Frederick's excitement, he forgot all about Mr. Makepeace and the beans and the peas and the little man dressed all in green. He was free of the orphanage. He followed Mr. Kimball, the solemn-looking man who had engaged him, through the gates and out into the streets of London.

Frederick knew he should not speak until he was spoken to. It was a rule. But as he walked beside Mr. Kimball through the crowded streets, he grew more and more impressed. At last, he could not keep the words inside a moment longer. "Surely London is the finest city in the world!"

"I agree." Mr. Kimball's long face changed completely when he turned to smile at Frederick. "And this the finest kingdom in the world."

As they walked along, Frederick marveled. London's streets were crowded with people from every walk of life, rich merchants to poor beggars, and lined with all manner of buildings, from crumbling slums to private homes as grand as any palace.

Mr. Kimball questioned Frederick now and then

about orphanage life as they made their way through the city. Frederick answered as best he could. The miles went quickly. Soon Mr. Kimball led him down a street that opened into a square with a neatly groomed park in the center. Ranged around the sides of the square so that each overlooked the park, fine stone houses, tall and narrow, stood shoulder to shoulder as if crowding for the best view.

"You will work there." Mr. Kimball gestured proudly to the finest house of all. "Schofield House."

Again Frederick marveled so much, he could not keep his words back. "It's enormous."

Mr. Kimball looked pleased. "It is the finest house in London."

They came to the front door of Schofield House. "Servants' entrance," said Mr. Kimball firmly. "We stay below stairs." Ignoring the great glossy door above, Frederick followed Mr. Kimball down a flight of steps to a door tucked into the areaway beneath.

Mr. Kimball brought Frederick into an entry with gleaming floor tiles and the delicious smell of boiling cabbage. They went through the servants' hall, Mr. Kimball pointing out the kitchen, pantry, and larder as they went. In the laundry room, which was spotless and warm from the fire heating the copper boiler, Mr. Kimball showed Frederick a simple bed in the corner. "You'll sleep here for now. The servants' quarters are at the top of the house, but we're pressed for space with the staff his lordship has engaged."

Frederick looked at Mr. Kimball to see if he meant it. Compared with the crowded, noisy sleeping quarters in the orphanage, the narrow bed seemed too good to be true. "I could sleep here? Alone?"

"Unless another lad is engaged," said Mr. Kimball. "Then the pair of you would be down here. We would find another straw mattress and a few more blankets, of course."

Half dazed by his good fortune, Frederick nodded.

"You'll do as you're told, promptly and well," said Mr. Kimball. "Try not to let yourself be seen by any of the family. If you are seen, it's unfortunate, but carry on with your work unless they ask you for something. Speak when you're spoken to and not before."

"Yes, sir." Frederick tried to take in his good fortune. He had a safe place to stay, even if it was in a wizard's house, and a bed both clean and warm. He had a position, honest employment. He was finding his way in the world. It had been a grand day, the grandest of Frederick's life so far, and all because he was the perfect size for a suit of livery.

∽

In the long days that followed, Frederick learned his way around the big house. The very first thing he was shown was a door he was ordered to avoid. It was on the ground floor at the back of the house, far away from the grand rooms where guests were entertained, and it was a very important door indeed.

"This is his lordship's workroom. Mind you keep away from it." Mr. Kimball scowled at Frederick. "That door is kept locked at all times. No one goes in without his lordship's consent. *No one*."

It looked to Frederick like a perfectly ordinary door. "Don't we clean the room and keep it tidy for him?"

"Don't you dare so much as touch the doorknob," Mr. Kimball said. "His lordship carries out his research in there." At Frederick's blank look, he added, "His magical studies."

"Magic?" Frederick remembered the gossip at the orphanage.

"Lord Schofield is a wizard. Thomas Schofield. The mysterious marquis, the gossips call him." Mr. Kimball rolled his eyes. "You've never even heard of him, have you?"

It did not seem like a good time to mention what the big boys had said about Lord Schofield grinding people's bones to make his bread. Frederick said, "Not really."

"Trust me, then. He's a very good wizard, respected by the king's own advisors at the Royal College of Wizards, but even the best of that lot have been known to be shockingly bad tempered," said Mr. Kimball. "He takes odd notions, his lordship does. So be careful. Mind what I tell you, now. Stay away."

Frederick kept a safe distance from the wizard's workroom. To annoy his new employer, a rich and powerful wizard, would be the last thing he wanted. If Frederick ever let his bones be ground up, Vardle would be very disappointed in him.

To Frederick, Schofield House was grand as a palace. The walls were hung with mirrors and paintings in great golden frames. The high ceilings were decorated with patterns of flowers and leaves and fruits and vines, all shaped out of pure white plaster. The windows were covered with curtains of silk, the borders touched with what looked like real gold. The floors were like yards and yards of polished bits of wood set at angles in a vast puzzle, and sometimes a big rug laid over it, woven in complicated patterns with shades of deep red and rich blue like a church window. The furniture was carved wood upholstered with silk in colors Frederick didn't even know words for. There were fat feather cushions embroidered with birds and flowers, all arranged just so on the chairs and settees.

Day by day, as he learned his duties, Frederick met the other servants on the staff. There were upper servants, who only served Lord and Lady Schofield personally, and there were lower servants, who worked for the upper servants as well as the Schofield family. The upper servants were far too grand to speak to the likes of Frederick except to give him orders. The lower servants seemed too busy looking down their noses at each other to notice Frederick even existed.

On Frederick's first morning at Schofield House, he met Bess the scullery maid as they were both waiting for breakfast. He soon learned that scullery maids did most of the dirty jobs around the house, scrubbing everything from kettles to the kitchen floor, but on that day, Frederick only knew that Bess was a brisk red-haired girl an inch taller than he was.

The cook, who was called Mr. Grant, had scraped the last of the porridge into the bowl for the girl ahead of him, so there was nothing left for Frederick. From his days at the orphanage Frederick knew what that meant—no breakfast for him. Dismayed, he turned away.

"Stay!" The girl caught his sleeve to stop him. She was at least a year older than he was, and strong enough to hold him fast. "Oats and groats, Mr. Grant, have mercy on him. He'll never get any bigger if he isn't fed properly."

"Oh, is it you that gives me orders now, little sauce-box?" The cook looked sharply from the girl to Frederick and back. "Or has the lad engaged you to represent him?"

"Grumpy, aren't we?" The girl handed her bowl to Frederick. "Here, have mine."

"No!" Frederick backed away from the bowl. At the orphanage he had long since learned that when someone offered to do someone else a good turn for what seemed like no reason, there was always a true reason, something unpleasant. But the girl was looking at him as if he had gone mad, so he did his best to explain himself. "I can't take that. What will you eat?"

"Oh, I shall beg a crust from somewhere," she said airily, "unless such grumpiness has become the custom of the kitchen."

"Never anything but sauce from you, lass. You should respect your elders." Mr. Grant seized a loaf of bread and cut a generous slice off the end. He held it out to Frederick. "I can't spare you a crumb more, so mind you don't whine for butter on it."

Frederick took the thick piece of bread and smelled it, marveling. "But it's still fresh." He had never known anyone to give away bread before it had turned as hard as a paving stone.

"It's yesterday's bread." Mr. Grant still sounded grumpy, but he had begun to look amused. "Any other complaints?"

"I'm not complaining." Frederick thanked first Mr. Grant and then the girl.

"Why are you thanking Bess?" Mr. Grant cut a slice

of cheese and gave it to Frederick. "She hasn't done anything. Get that inside you, boy."

Frederick thanked him again. "If you ever need your knives sharpened, I'll be glad to do it for you. I have the knack of it, I've been told."

"Do you, now? I'll bear it in mind." Mr. Grant turned to the girl. "What are the pair of you standing about for? I gave you that food to eat, not to admire. Off with you."

When they were safely out of the cook's way, Frederick thanked Bess again. "I don't know how to repay you."

"Just a taste of that cheese would do so nicely," said the girl.

"I'm Frederick Lincoln. I'm the new footboy."

"I know. I'm Bess Parker. I work for Fan mostly. She's the laundress. Trade you some of this porridge for a bit of your cheese?"

∾

Frederick soon discovered how lucky he was to have Bess to show him how to go on in the great household. She had several aunts and cousins on the staff, and her younger brother, Clarence, although not yet in the employ of the household as a regular servant, sometimes helped to scrub the floors and clean the boots.

"Clarence doesn't say much," Bess told Frederick, "but he is a right one. Aren't you, Clarence?"

The three of them were scrubbing the last faint traces of grime out of the dimmest corners of the laundry. Clarence only nodded and kept scrubbing.

"He's only eight, and he looks younger still, for he's a bit undersized. But when he's grown a bit, Mr. Kimball promised our pa he will give him the chance of a place on the staff." Bess went back to scrubbing. "Mr. Kimball keeps his promises."

Frederick tried to get Clarence to talk, but although he was friendly enough, he would only nod yes or shake his head no in answer to questions.

"He's a bit bashful," Bess explained. "You're new here. And we don't want Fan to catch us chattering instead of working. That would never do."

"Keep a silent tongue in a wise head." Frederick rinsed his brush and started scrubbing the next corner. "That's what Vardle at the orphanage used to say. He says it's a good thing for a servant not to talk much."

"That's me out, then." Bess scraped a stubborn spot with her thumbnail. "We aren't supposed to speak to Lord or Lady Schofield unless they speak to us first. Sometimes I think I may burst. I'd have a dreadful time if I wasn't to speak at all. I talk a lot. I like it."

"Lucky for me you do. I have a lot to learn. There's

Fan, for one." Frederick kept his head down, scrubbing hard while he risked speaking honestly. "She scares me."

"No need to be frightened," Bess assured him. "But you'd do well to respect her. When Fan tells you to hop, you hop it. If you sauce her, she'll box your ears so hard they'll sting for two days." She mimed a slap to the side of Frederick's head to show him what she meant, but she was just teasing.

Out of habit, Frederick ducked anyway. "Fan doesn't tell me anything. She doesn't speak to me at all, just points to show what she wants me to carry. Why won't she talk to me?"

"Oh, she's still fussed over the last bootboy. Georgie came from the orphanage too."

"Georgie Biddle?" Frederick moved his bucket and began on a fresh bit of grimy floor.

Bess nodded. "Nasty piece of work."

"What happened to Georgie? Did the wizard grind his bones to make his bread?"

Bess burst out laughing. "Did he what? No! Lord Schofield's not that sort of wizard at all. He's a bit strange perhaps, but he's not a cannibal. What gave you that notion?"

Frederick felt embarrassed. "That's what they said at the orphanage. Did Fan do something to him? Did he do something to Fan?"

"Nothing like that. Fat Georgie stole a silver tea-spoon from the dining room."

"So Mr. Kimball sacked him?"

"No, Georgie ran away before they could dismiss him. Left his livery, or they'd have claimed he stole that as well." Bess sounded bored. "Just as well he left it, or you wouldn't be wearing it now. It looks better on you than it did on him. Strange, when you're so much skinnier."

Frederick tried to look down at himself but bumped his bucket and almost overturned it. Bess steadied it for him. "Don't worry about your looks, Frederick. It's just a matter of time. You'll have to go on working hard until Fan notices you aren't a thief."

"That I can do." With satisfaction, Frederick gazed at the expanse of freshly scrubbed floor all around them. "We're nearly finished."

"Finished here, maybe. We are to clean the still room next." Bess pointed to the far corner of the laundry. "Clarence, you've missed a spot."

Something cold seemed to squeeze Frederick's stomach as memories of darkness and hunger returned. "The still room? You have one here?"

"Of course we do. Every proper household has a still room," Bess declared. "Where else do you make potions and lotions and things that smell good?"

"What do you mean?" Frederick could not conceal

his confusion. "The still room is where you have to be still. That's where they lock you up for punishment."

Bess and Clarence regarded Frederick in silence. They exchanged a wordless look of concern. Then Clarence took Frederick's hand as Bess said, "I'll show you."

Still holding his scrub brush, Frederick let Clarence lead him as they trailed after Bess. Down the corridor and around a corner, they came to a spacious, well-lit room furnished with shelves and a worktable. In every corner hung bunches of dried herbs. Fascinating smells came from the bottles and crocks, all neatly ranked and labeled, on every side.

"This is a proper still room," said Bess. "I don't know what sort of carryings-on there were at that orphanage of yours, but in a proper still room, things are distilled and preserved."

Frederick looked around, marveling. "No beetles."

"I should hope not!" Bess's sharp eyes were already measuring the task before them. "Clarence, fetch us the bucket."

IN WHICH FREDERICK LEAVES
HIS WORK UNFINISHED

Working hard came easily to Frederick. He did as he was told. He used his head about the things he wasn't told. Before long, Frederick's readiness to work wore Fan's suspicions away. The laundress grew used to Frederick and began to give him orders. Lots of orders. Frederick ran upstairs and down with folded stacks of clean linen and armfuls of dirty linen. He carried messages and delivered orders for supplies. Fan needed not just soap but starch and washing blue to do her work properly.

One day when Frederick was sent to the chemist's to fetch an order, he was kept waiting a long time— long enough to notice a sheet almanac posted on the wall. By the time the order was ready, Frederick had worked out from the calendar that it must be the twentieth of April. That meant it was the day after his eleventh birthday. He was sure about the date because it had been listed in the orphanage registry. Vardle had helped him find it out. The cook had taken great pride in telling Frederick all about his adventures back in 1809, feeding the Royal Navy when Frederick was only a squalling infant.

"I'm eleven," Frederick told Bess, on his return with the washing blue he'd been sent for. "I was eleven years old yesterday."

"Many happy returns," said Bess. "Fan, yesterday was Frederick's birthday."

At first, Fan only grumbled over the quality of the washing blue he had brought her, but when she had it put safely away among her supplies, Fan told Frederick, "When Kimball lets you have your next change of linen, give me that shirt and I'll clean and press it for you. I'll show you how to tie your cravat properly as well. It's a disgrace the way you wear it now. You might as well tie a great bandage around your neck."

A few days later, Mr. Kimball gave Frederick a second shirt and two more white cravats along with an advance on his first quarter's wages. Frederick took Fan up on her offer, and she washed and ironed his shirt for him.

"You want to use the smoothing iron like this," Fan instructed as Frederick watched her press his clean cravat. She folded the crisp fabric so that only the center section was the full width. Each end was made long and narrow when she folded the fabric in thirds and pressed the edges sharp.

"Now, stand up straight." Fan stood behind Frederick and placed the center of the cravat against his Adam's apple, wrapping the cravat ends around so they crossed at the back of his neck, and then draping them so they hung down in front of him. "Hold it in place for me. One finger will do. Now, look at the ceiling."

Fan showed Frederick how she wanted him to keep the cloth still while she walked around in front of him and studied the fall of the fabric. "Keep your chin up, no matter what happens. This is the tricky bit," she told him. Then, without fumbling or hesitation, she seized the two ends and knotted them deftly under Frederick's chin. She did something to the ends to tuck them in neatly, then stood back and studied the result.

"Drop your chin," Fan ordered. "That's right. Look at me."

Frederick brought his gaze down from the ceiling to Fan's critical inspection. He felt as if he might be choking.

"You'll do," said Fan at last. "Mind, if I had to adjust it, I'd take the whole thing off and start again with a fresh cravat. You can't make a bad sauce good by adding more eggs. Once they curdle, you must throw the whole lot out and start fresh."

"Is this thing supposed to be strangling me?" Frederick managed to ask.

"Are you suffering for fashion? You'll get used to it," Fan said heartlessly. "Next time you're upstairs, use a looking glass. Once you see how fine it makes you look, you'll be after me for lessons."

Frederick knew better than to argue. The next opportunity that came, he looked himself over in the first mirror he found. The cravat did make him look more elegant, but he didn't think it could be quite right, wearing so much fabric wrapped around his neck. It looked like someone had tried to cut off his head and then fasten it back on with bandages.

That night, when Frederick unwound his cravat and readied the clean one he would put on next morning, he used the smoothing iron to duplicate the folds Fan had made. He did his best to copy her work, but next morning, somehow it looked different. The ends were a trifle more narrow, the edges a trifle more crisp.

Frederick tied his cravat with care, and even though it was not quite a duplicate of the fashion Fan had shown him, it felt better around his neck and looked far neater. He could breathe and turn his head freely. When next he studied himself in the looking glass, he discovered that he looked as elegant as any footman, not bandaged at all.

⌒

Frederick's first glimpse of his employer came when he was scrubbing floors near the forbidden workroom. He was scraping at a stubborn spot when the door opened behind him and slammed shut.

"Confound it! Kate, have you seen my sealing wax?"

Frederick turned to look and froze in place so he wouldn't be noticed. He knew without being told that he was looking at his employer. Who else would dare use the workroom?

The wizard marched away, but even from behind Frederick could see the man was stocky, and much too short to be a stately butler or even a fashionable footman. He didn't look a bit like a wizard. He was mumbling to himself wildly and running his hands through his hair, making it stand on end, as if he were some sort of a madman.

As Frederick watched him go, the wizard called out again. "Kate!"

From around the corner, a lady in a beautiful pink gown joined him. Her dark hair was twisted up in a complex knot at the back of her head, but the smudge of ink on her nose rather spoiled the elegant effect. She took the wizard's arm as if joining him for a stroll. "Of course I haven't, Thomas. I have my own, after all. Would you care to use some of mine?"

"I don't know. Is it red?" The pair of them turned the corner and Frederick went back to work. It was a great relief. Wizards were nothing like what he'd expected. His employer was just like anyone else, only rich.

~

Nearly every day, Frederick learned a new skill as he went about his work. Under the watchful eyes of Mr. Kimball and of Mrs. Dutton the housekeeper, Frederick had learned how to dust. The very first thing to know about dusting turned out to be *wash your hands.*

"Use plenty of soap when you scrub your hands," Mrs. Dutton commanded. "I won't have nice things made nasty by prints from greasy fingers. Clean and trim your fingernails while you are about it. You're not a gardener, after all. Let the dirt go."

Mrs. Dutton ordered Frederick to start at the top and work downward, told him when to use the duster and when to employ the whisk broom, and set him to work.

Frederick's favorite part of his job was dusting and waxing and polishing the furniture. The wood carvings seemed almost grateful for the beeswax polish he rubbed in with fingertips and cloth. The beeswax was scented with lavender, and in the quiet of the drawing room, the clean smell of it filled Frederick with peace.

Sometimes it was so quiet, all Frederick heard was

the ticking of the tall clock in the corner, the one it was Mr. Kimball's duty to wind.

Sometimes it was so peaceful, Frederick felt he might be dreaming. Sometimes his ears buzzed a little, so that he almost thought he heard dry leaves rustling. There were no leaves to be found, of course, nor anything else in the room to explain the noise, but when Frederick heard that sound, he felt an odd sense of companionship, as if someone friendly was nearby, just out of sight. Sometimes, at his dreamiest, Frederick even thought he detected a low humming, as if there were bees about. Embroidered bees to go with the embroidered flowers, he told himself, and laughed.

After polishing furniture, Frederick's favorite task was cleaning knives. Sometimes he was even permitted to sharpen a few of the knives Mr. Grant the cook used. Mr. Grant was as different from Vardle as the food he prepared was different from orphanage food. At the orphanage, what little they were given to eat was usually cold and often tasted bad. At Schofield House, even in the servants' hall, the food was so good that sometimes Frederick wanted to sing.

Jolly round Vardle had taken pride in everything he cooked. Even if it could scarcely be scraped out of the pot, he was pleased with his work. "Fit for the Royal Navy," he would say. Skinny Mr. Grant, on the other hand, was as stern as a judge about what came out of his kitchen. Often grumpy over flaws no one else could find in the food he prepared, Mr. Grant made sure everything he cooked was the best he could make it. When he praised Frederick for the way he sharpened the knives, Frederick was proud. He knew he must have done his work perfectly.

The only tasks Frederick truly disliked were emptying chamber pots and blacking boots. Even though he disliked blacking boots, he did it beautifully, for Frederick knew the first rule of polishing. It worked for boots just as it did for anything else. Before one could even begin, the boots must be clean. Handling the blacking was a dirty job, and it always took a long time to buff the leather to the proper perfect shine.

One wet night, Frederick sat by the laundry room fire, cleaning mud off a pair of Lord Schofield's leather boots. Lord Schofield must have visited a very low part of town, for the filth caked on the leather smelled dreadful. Frederick knew that the best way to deal with mud was to wait for it to dry, but this mud would not be dry by morning, when the boots would be called for. No, it was scrub and oil for him.

First Frederick used saddle soap to clean the boots and then neat's-foot oil to keep the leather from cracking after it had dried. By the time he was finished, his fingers stung, and the boots, although clean, still needed to be polished before they were returned to Lord Schofield's valet, Piers. Frederick set the clean boots beside the fire to dry a bit more before he started with the blacking and buffing, but the long day caught up with him. His task only half done, Frederick dozed off.

Somewhere far into the night, Frederick woke confused. It took him a moment to remember why he was sleeping beside the hearth instead of in his own straw bed. When at last the memory of his unfinished task came back to him, Frederick looked around for the boots. To his surprise, Lord Schofield's boots were right beside him, ready and waiting. Close examination showed Frederick that the boots were not only perfectly clean and perfectly dry, inside and out, but they had been polished with such care that the gloss of the leather rivaled a looking glass.

For a moment, as he inspected the boots, a soft rustle that was almost, but not quite, the sound of a breeze moving dry leaves, filled the room. Frederick dropped the boots and gazed wildly around. The rustling stopped. Nothing was there to account for the sound.

Nowhere did Frederick find a hint to tell him who had done his work for him. Even his buffing rags and boot brushes were dry, untouched by any signs of recent use.

Frederick put more coal on the fire and sat between the hearth and the boots for the rest of the night, but he could not reason out what had happened.

First thing in the morning he delivered the boots to Lord Schofield's valet, Piers, and spent the rest of his time scrubbing the laundry floor. He asked Fan, Bess, Clarence, and everyone else he encountered, about the polished boots. No one knew a thing about it.

"You did it in your sleep," said Bess. "Clarence used to walk in his sleep something chronic."

Clarence just shook his head and went on scrubbing the floor.

"How could I have done it in my sleep?" Frederick showed Bess his hands, chapped but clean, front and back. "Wouldn't my hands show the boot blacking?"

"Must have been a brownie did it then," said Bess. "Mind you don't thank him, or he will run away and never come back."

"No brownies or hobgoblins here," said Fan. "Even if his lordship wasn't more than a match for such things, his mother would never have stood for such doings in her household. I've known folk who had the brownie in their house plug the chimney with a feather pillow it hauled into its nest. Worse than badgers, they can be. Worse than bats, even."

"Badgers and bats, my Sunday hat," said Bess. "Those boots were polished, weren't they? Someone did it. It wasn't a ghost."

"Someone did it," agreed Fan, "and all in good time we'll find out who it was."

The next night, Frederick lay wondering in the dark. For the first time in a long time, he thought about the dream he'd had in the orphanage kitchen, the deep soft voice counting out the peas and beans. Had there been a voice the night before, a deep drowsy voice? Had that voice said something about corn and rye? Frederick fell asleep still wondering. Somewhere in the night, it came back to him, no dream at all, but the clear memory of a deep voice. *"Peas and beans, corn and rye. Who can work like Billy Bly?"*

IN WHICH FREDERICK
MEETS HIS FIRST WIZARD

Next morning, the summons came. Mr. Kimball came looking for Frederick and when he found him, seized him by the ear. "You are wanted in the drawing room. Lord Schofield wishes to ask you some questions. You will tell him what he desires to know. You will tell him at once, do you understand?"

Frederick had to balance on the very tips of his toes to ease the pain in his ear. "Yes, sir! Right away, sir!" As Mr. Kimball hauled him along, Frederick examined his conscience and his fingernails, but he couldn't think of anything he'd done wrong. Nothing, that is, except fall asleep with his work half done. Could that be a bone-grinding offense?

Lord Schofield dismissed Mr. Kimball with a gesture and Frederick found himself alone in the drawing room with his employer.

"You're Frederick Lincoln? From the orphanage?" The wizard stood before the window. The light behind him made it hard to see his expression.

"Yes, my lord. Mr. Kimball engaged me, my lord," Frederick replied, mouth so dry with fear his lips tried to stick together when he said the *m*'s.

Lord Schofield paced to the far end of the room and returned. When he paused to study Frederick, Frederick had his first good look at his employer's face. Lord Schofield did not seem any more like a lord than he did like a wizard. He had dark eyes and dark hair, but that was not unusual. So did Frederick. He still looked exactly like anybody else, well dressed, but no dandy. The only unusual things about him were his waistcoat, which was vivid blue silk embroidered with a pattern of peacock feathers, and the sharpness of his eyes.

"Have you brought anything with you from the orphanage?" Lord Schofield asked at last. "Any luggage?"

Frederick made himself speak plainly despite his nerves. "Didn't have nothing—" He caught himself. "I mean, I had nothing to bring, my lord."

"Nothing whatever?" Lord Schofield looked keenly interested. "Not even a hat? A pair of gloves? A family keepsake of some kind, perhaps?"

"Don't have family keepsakes when you're an orphan." Frederick felt pinned by Lord Schofield's gaze and found it took all his resolve to look steadily back.

The wizard's sharp eyes didn't waver. "Silly of me. Of course you don't. What do you have?"

"Mr. Kimball let me wear the suit of livery he had me put on, my lord," Frederick replied. "He engaged me because he thought it fit me best."

"Just so. Unlike so many, you know how to wear a cravat. Rare in someone your age. Of any age, come to that. Commendable." Lord Schofield tugged at the cravat tied around his own neck and cleared his throat. "Tell me about this orphanage. How did you come to be there?

"It all happened before I can remember, so I only know what I've been told," said Frederick. "The orphanage at Lincoln's Inn is much the same as any other orphanage, I am sure. I was sent there when me mum—my mother—died having my baby sister. My baby sister died too."

Lord Schofield looked grave. "No other family?"
Frederick shook his head.

"What of your father?"

"Don't know as I had ever one, my lord. Will that be all, my lord?"

"No, it will not be all." Lord Schofield gazed piercingly at Frederick, as if he were trying to see right through him. "I wish to ask you to assist me with an experiment. Do you have any objection?"

"What sort of experiment?" Frederick asked, then coughed and added hastily, "I mean, no, my lord. No objection, that is."

Lord Schofield regarded Frederick with approval. "It is only good sense for you to inquire. The experiment I have in mind will not harm you in the least. If what you have told me is true, we will be finished in five minutes, and I suspect it will seem to you to have been an utter waste of both your time and mine."

Although very much against the idea of helping a wizard do anything, Frederick couldn't think of any safe way to refuse. "Very well, my lord."

Lord Schofield turned for the door. "I shall conduct the experiment in my study. Follow me. Don't speak unless you must, and at all costs, don't touch *anything*."

⌒

Together, Frederick and his employer made their way to Lord Schofield's workroom. As his lordship unlocked the forbidden door and let them into the room where he did his wizardry, Frederick felt a thrill of excitement.

It was a spacious room, lit by a large brass lamp like a turnip with tentacles. The floor was bare. Except for a long table in the center of the room, there was hardly any furniture. The walls were lined with shelves of books and scientific equipment. If he closed his eyes, Frederick had the sense the room was crowded, as if there was a party going on just outside of his range of hearing.

Marveling, Frederick let his gaze travel around and around the room. On the shelves with the books he recognized a clock, a set of scales, a globe, and what looked like a lizard in a green glass jar.

Frederick knew it was wrong to point, but he couldn't stop himself. "What's that?"

Lord Schofield finished lighting the lamps. "I told you not to speak unless you must."

"But what is that thing?"

Lord Schofield sighed. "Once it was a lizard. Now it is merely a travel souvenir. If you have no further questions, I will begin. Stand over there. Don't move. Don't say another word until I tell you that you may."

Frederick took his place near the table and watched in fascination as Lord Schofield drew a circle around Frederick with a bit of blue chalk, muttering the whole time. When the circle was complete, Lord Schofield made another circle, far smaller, a few feet away. Then he put the chalk on the table, held one hand in the air, put the other in his pocket, and said some words Frederick didn't understand.

Frederick's ears popped and abruptly the smaller circle was no longer empty. Standing inside it was a creature like a grumpy little man, hardly up to Frederick's knee, dressed all in green.

"Ow." The little man glared at Lord Schofield. "I was asleep, you know. No call to haul me out of a sound sleep." His voice was as deep as the hum of bees.

"Sorry," said Lord Schofield, without sounding apologetic in the least. "Not such a waste of time after all, it seems. Do you know this fellow? You may speak now, Frederick."

Frederick rubbed his eyes and took a long look. It was the little man he'd dreamed of, no question. He thought carefully about the question he had been asked. Lord Schofield was nothing like as cross as Mr. Makepeace had been. But still, dreaming of the little man was not the same as knowing him. "My lord, we have not been formally introduced."

"Oh, haven't you?" Lord Schofield turned his attention to the little man. "Do you know this young chop-logic, fellow?"

The little man studied Frederick with interest. "I might."

"Suppose you introduce yourself to him properly, then," said Lord Schofield.

"Suppose I don't?" the little man replied. "Names are powerful things. I don't introduce myself lightly."

"Don't you, indeed?" Lord Schofield moved his hand in the air.

"Ow!" The little man rubbed his left elbow. "That pinches, you know." To Frederick, he said, "My name is Billy Bly."

Frederick studied the little man before he answered. Billy Bly gave him back look for look, bright and friendly. Frederick trusted him at once. He reminded himself to be careful and go slowly. He was almost sure Billy Bly had saved him from a day locked in the orphanage still room, but he had been wrong about trusting people before. "How do you do?" Frederick gave the little man a polite bow. "My name is Frederick Lincoln."

Billy Bly looked pleased. "Very civil of you, I'm sure."

Hesitantly, Frederick went on. "Did we meet at the orphanage? I seem to remember seeing you once before. In the kitchen there."

"I know. Vardle wasn't so bad, though the things he did to good honest food ought to be a crime. He meant well. But that Makepeace was a right swine, wasn't he? How did he ever come by a good name like that? He should be called something far more like his nature." Billy Bly made a very rude noise. "Something like that. Horrible man."

"You helped me sort the peas and beans," Frederick said. He opened his mouth to thank the little man, but Lord Schofield held up an index finger to hush him.

"Think carefully before you speak," Lord Schofield

advised. "Fellows like Billy Bly sometimes react with unexpected violence to being thanked for their help. If he is under a spell, it may free him. Beware. Brownies can be unpredictable."

"*Are* you under a spell?" Frederick asked Billy Bly.

"Thank you for your kind concern, I'm sure. As it happens, I'm not. Though if I *were* under a spell," Billy Bly added, with a superior glance at Lord Schofield, "I wouldn't be allowed to say."

"Then I thank you for your help," said Frederick. "And did you black the boots as well?"

Billy Bly beamed at Frederick. "Not bad, eh?"

"Perfect," said Frederick. "I never saw leather with such a shine. I wish you'd show me how to do it."

"If he hadn't made those boots shine so, I might not have noticed he was here. At least not until this came to my attention." From a silver tray on his worktable, Lord Schofield picked up a blackened rag.

To Frederick's horror, he recognized that the black rag had once been one of the fine damask napkins used by the guests who dined with his lordship. Now it was crumpled and stained with what looked very much like boot polish.

Billy Bly took no notice of the rag. "Yes, I noticed the protective charms you and your family have put on the place," he said airily. "Nice work indeed. Very sound, very workmanlike."

"Very rude of you to ignore them." Lord Schofield sounded nettled.

"It was never my intention," said Billy Bly, "to be rude. It is less than polite, some folk might point out, to set charms on your house to keep folk like me at a distance. Condemned without a hearing, you might say."

"You might say so, but as it is my house, I would not," said Lord Schofield. "Did you come to us from the same orphanage young Frederick did?"

"That's right," said Billy Bly. "Been there for years. I was among the students, barristers, and benchers next door at Lincoln's Inn for years before that."

Lord Schofield looked amused. "No doubt that's where you picked up your legal education."

The question seemed to make Billy Bly cross. "If you mean I am a stickler for rules, that's right. I also like a place with plenty of interest, lots of things happening. Splendid grub, too."

"If life there suited you so well, why leave?" asked Lord Schofield.

"The usual story." Billy Bly sighed. "Too much of a good thing. The place attracted a low element, hobgoblins no better than scaff and raff. They fought over scraps."

"So you moved on in search of better neighbors?" Lord Schofield guessed. "Before they moved you out by force?"

"No competition to speak of at the orphanage," Billy Bly agreed. "No surprise there. The cooking was so bad, the mice complained."

"Why did you stay?" Frederick asked. "If it's good food you like, the orphanage was no place for you."

"That swine Makepeace." Billy Bly looked embarrassed. "His favorite amusement was punishing you orphans. There he was spilling beans and then ordering you boys to pick up after him, or to put things in order by size, or to count them. Counting is my favorite. Once I've begun a task like that, I have to finish it. It's not my fault, it's the way I'm made. I could no more walk away from counting mustard seeds than I could walk into a church on Easter morning."

"Then why did you leave?" Frederick asked, more puzzled than ever.

If possible, Billy Bly looked even more embarrassed. "You seemed a nice lad," he said at last. "When you flitted, I thought I'd flit with you, see you were looked after properly."

Frederick was horrified to feel his throat tighten with tears. Except for Vardle perhaps, no one had ever cared tuppence whether Frederick had been looked after properly or thrown in the river. He could hardly keep from showing how much the little man's words meant to him. "That—that was very kind of you."

"The pleasure was all mine," said Billy Bly. "The

food here is far better, and whatever his shortcomings, the cook here knows when to put down a nice saucer of cream and look the other way."

"Oh, he does, does he?" Lord Schofield looked thoughtful. "I can see I'll have to have a chat with Grant about that. You have done very little damage during your stay here. I commend you for your restraint. But I know the ways of brownies and hobgoblins too well to believe that can go on for long."

"You may dock the cost of the napkin from my wages," Frederick said. "It was my fault for falling asleep before my work was done."

Lord Schofield looked a little sad. "Billy Bly helps you with your work. He came with you from the orphanage. If he leaves, will you leave with him?"

With a pang, Frederick thought of his clean clothes and his comfortable bed. He thought of the food, good and plentiful, and the pleasure and pride he took in earning a steady wage. "Must I go?"

"That's for you to decide. But go Billy Bly must. I don't blame either of you for ruining the napkin. You didn't do it and he couldn't help it. That's his nature. Hobgoblins make chancy houseguests. Next time he may take it into his head to clean the chimneys with a featherbed."

A little desperately, Frederick said, "If he does, I'll pay for the damages."

"Your wages won't cover the damage a hobgoblin can do," said Lord Schofield. "A brownie took a liking to my brother, Edward, when we were both boys. Every plant the gardener set out would turn up in Edward's room sooner or later, in every container you can imagine, from shoes to chamber pots. By the time my mother banished him from our house in the country, that creature had the whole place turned upside down."

"What if Billy Bly promised not to do any damage? What if he swore?"

"Wouldn't swear," said Billy Bly. "Wouldn't promise."

"You may keep your position, Frederick. But the brownie must go." Lord Schofield lifted both hands in the air. "No hard feelings, Billy Bly."

"None at all, your bossiness," Billy Bly replied. To Frederick, he said, "Mind how you go, lad."

Lord Schofield moved his hands in a quick, graceful gesture. Frederick's ears popped again, and the chalk circle was empty. Billy Bly was gone as if Frederick had dreamed the whole thing; nothing remaining of his presence but the fading sound of dry leaves rustling from every direction.

"That's that." Lord Schofield dusted his hands. "You may scrub the floor now, Frederick."

With a sense of chill disbelief heavy in his stomach,

Frederick fetched a bucket of water and a brush. Carefully he scrubbed the chalk marks off the study floor. While he cleaned up after the very first magic spell he had ever seen cast, Lord Schofield wrote notes in a big leather-bound book.

So finally he knew, Frederick told himself. It was no dream. Billy Bly had been as real as Mr. Vardle. Now Billy Bly was gone. The empty feeling soaked into him the way the cold water soaked his knees as he worked.

Now Frederick was alone in Schofield House, lonely in a way he'd never been before. He was used to feeling alone. But he wished he had known Billy Bly had been there. Frederick would have asked Billy Bly a thousand questions, trying to learn everything there was to know about brownies and hobgoblins. More even than the lost chance to learn, Frederick mourned the loss of his unseen companion. He wished, more than anything, that he'd known someone in the world had cared about him enough to follow him from the orphanage. Too late. In a house full of people, Frederick found himself alone.

IN WHICH FREDERICK
GOES UP IN THE WORLD

From the day he banished Billy Bly from Schofield House, Lord Schofield took an interest in Frederick. He already behaved to everyone as if the work they did for him was important, and he never seemed to notice there was a rule that the servants should not speak to him unless he had spoken to them first. In Frederick's case, Lord Schofield added curiosity to his usual courtesy.

"You haven't seen anything of Billy Bly since I sent him away?" Lord Schofield asked, almost daily. "You would mention it if you had, I hope?"

Sometimes Frederick would listen hard as he polished furniture, but he never heard leaves rustling, nor ever felt the slightest sense of unseen companionship. "No, my lord," he assured his employer. "Of course I would, my lord."

"Excellent, Frederick. Good work. Keep it up."

Frederick was unsettled by Lord Schofield's air of friendly interest. Since he had explained about the business with Billy Bly to Bess first chance he had, he asked Bess for her opinion while they were scrubbing the kitchen floor together.

"No mystery there," Bess said. "Magic is the one thing Lord Schofield truly cares about in this world, right?"

Frederick knew no such thing, but he could tell from Bess's voice what the answer was supposed to be, so he echoed, "Right."

"What is this Billy Bly thing?" Bess demanded.

"Magic." Frederick was in no doubt whatsoever about that.

"Right. So why was Billy Bly here?"

"Because of me?" Frederick ventured.

"Right. Now, why is Lord Schofield keeping you under his eye?"

"Because Billy Bly liked me?" Frederick asked.

Bess rapped his knuckles with her scrub brush, but not very hard. "Because you brought him with you, fool. Lord Schofield wants to know why, and what else you may have brought with you without knowing."

"But I didn't even notice Billy Bly was here," Frederick protested. "Or at the orphanage, for that matter." But he had noticed at the orphanage, Frederick reminded himself. He just hadn't understood what it was he had noticed.

"Don't go all pie-faced worrying over it. Lord Schofield is curious as a cat. Billy Bly made him curious about you. That's all. Don't worry. He'll lose interest soon enough." Bess went back to scrubbing.

In a way, she was quite wrong about Lord Schofield. He didn't lose interest in Frederick. But in a way she was quite right, for Lord Schofield *was* as curious as a cat. The thing that most interested Lord Schofield about Frederick was the way he tied his cravat.

"You look remarkably tidy on a daily basis, and I know for a fact you can't have more than two neck cloths to your name. How do you manage it?" Lord Schofield demanded when next they met. "It takes Piers an hour and a dozen neck cloths every morning, and if I'm not to go out looking like a badly made bed, I have to tie the thing myself."

"It's just a knack. Sometimes I have to find a looking glass," Frederick admitted.

Lord Schofield frowned at Frederick's cravat. "There's more to it than a knack. Explain the trick of it to Piers."

The very next morning, Frederick presented himself to Piers in his lordship's dressing room.

"Lord Schofield sent me," Frederick said.

Piers, a well-scrubbed, muscular young man, looked

up from reading his lordship's morning newspaper. "Ah, young Frederick. Yes, I was told to expect you. You're to give me lessons in how to tie a cravat properly."

"If you please, sir," said Frederick politely. "Lord Schofield's orders."

Piers sighed as he folded the newspaper away. "You can save it. I haven't the aptitude."

"How do you know?" Frederick asked. "You haven't tried."

"Oh, haven't I?" Piers looked gloomy. "Dozens of neck cloths I've spoiled doing it wrong. They wrinkle if I so much as look at them. Fan won't even speak to me anymore."

"Did Fan show you how it's done?" Frederick asked. "All I know is what she showed me."

"She tried a few times." Piers shook his head. "Lord Schofield's orders, of course. But it's no use. I ruin them every time."

"Let me show you, just once," said Frederick, "so we can honestly say we tried."

"Just once, then." With another sigh Piers opened a drawer and drew out a crisp clean neck cloth, neatly folded. As he handed it to Frederick, he was already undoing his own cravat. "Have at it, lad."

Frederick shook out the neck cloth and put the valet's smoothing iron to heat in the fireplace. He cleared a place among the brushes and razors on his lordship's dressing table and folded a towel to serve as a pressing cloth. When the iron was hot, Frederick smoothed the ends of the neck cloth as if it were his own, then positioned Piers before the dressing room's looking glass.

"Now, watch me." Frederick worked as quickly as he could, given that Piers was so tall he had to climb on a chair at times to get the angle right. Deftly, Frederick twisted and folded the fabric around Piers's neck. "Look up at the ceiling. Hold still."

Piers tilted his head back meekly. Frederick made the final adjustments and tied the knot just so. He let the folds of cloth go where they wanted to go, soft but not too soft, crisp but not too crisp.

"Now lower your jaw as you bring your head forward so that the fabric squashes down and the folds turn out properly." Frederick surveyed the result with disfavor. "If we do this again, I shall fetch a step stool. You're too tall."

"No need." Entranced, Piers was gazing at himself in the looking glass. "Frederick—you're a marvel." He turned his head this way and that, admiring his cravat. "How smart I look. Hang on a moment." He left the dressing room abruptly.

By the time Piers returned, Frederick had finished clearing up the dressing room. "If you want a step stool, I'll build you one. I've spoken to Lord Schofield, young Frederick. You are now officially the assistant valet. You shall tie his lordship's cravats for him from now on."

"Assistant valet?" echoed Frederick. "Me?"

"That's right. He's even agreed to increase your wages." Piers glanced around the room and beamed at how tidy it was. "Your new duties begin at once. Tie his lordship's cravat."

"Now?" Frederick put the smoothing iron back in the fire to heat. "This instant?"

Shaved and dressed, Lord Schofield strolled into the dressing room in his shirtsleeves. "This instant. Why not?"

Frederick couldn't think of any reason why not, so he set to work preparing his lordship's neck cloth. It took longer than usual, for Frederick was determined not to blunder. He worked with his lightest touch, making the edges of the neck cloth smooth and sharp as the blade of a knife.

"Look up at the ceiling and hold still, my lord," said Frederick, when it was time. He tied the knot and tweaked the fabric into place. "Now, lower your chin." Soon Lord Schofield was wearing a properly tied cravat.

For once in his life lost for words, Lord Schofield spent fully five minutes studying his reflection in the looking glass. Then he clapped Frederick on the shoulder and shook his hand. "I'd no idea you were so deft, lad. Well done!"

Frederick, speechless with happiness at such praise, could only hold out Lord Schofield's jacket. Lord Schofield slid into it and slapped Piers on the back. "It's official. You now have an assistant valet, Piers. A better life for all of us."

Lord Schofield confirmed his new position with Mr. Kimball at once. The butler made certain Frederick knew every detail of his new position. Frederick would still clean his lordship's boots, but only his lordship's, not the rest of the household. There would be no more chamber pots, except for his lordship's, and no more scrubbing of floors. He didn't have to sleep among the upper servants, as they were still pressed for room, so Frederick chose to keep his bed in the laundry, where the fire made things cozy and hot water was plentiful.

Bess heard the gossip of his good news before he had a chance to tell her, and she congratulated him on his good fortune. Bess had good news of her own. "Now that the season is ending, his lordship is going to spend the rest of the year in the country." Bess threw her arms around Frederick and spun them both in a circle. "So are we! Isn't that grand? We're going to the country!"

"The country?" Frederick repeated blankly. "What country?"

Bess stopped hugging Frederick and shook him

briskly. "This country, silly. Mr. Kimball was allowed to choose which of us servants stay here and which come along to Skeynes, and we are among those who are to go."

"Skeynes?" Frederick echoed.

"Yes, the Schofields' estate, Skeynes. It was ever so grand there once, and I don't care what anyone says. It will be grand again." Bess bounced a little more in sheer excitement.

Frederick thought it over. "Just us? Must be a lot of work, moving to a new house."

"What is wrong with you, Frederick? You aren't usually such a goose. Quite half the staff is coming," said Bess. "We're to go on ahead to be sure the house is fit before Lord and Lady Schofield's arrival. And it's not a new house, but an old one. It has been neglected in the past few years, but before that it was as elegant as anything."

"Wait a moment. How many houses does his lordship have?" Frederick asked.

Bess hesitated, counting on her fingers, then waved the question aside. "Dozens, I suppose. But he only lives in a few of them."

"A *few*? You can only live in one place, surely? Why have more than one house?"

"For the income," Bess replied. "Rents and leases and all that sort of thing."

"Oh, I understand." Frederick thought it over. "If this Skeynes place is so wonderful, why does his lordship live here and not there? Why was it neglected?"

Bess lowered her voice. "All I know is, his lordship's older brother died there. The whole family took against the place. Wouldn't set foot there. But ever since he and her ladyship returned from their wedding journey, his lordship has had men busy repairing the place. My aunt who lives near there says it's been years they've been at it. The work is finished at last, so Mr. Kimball says. When the season is over, we're to go."

"Which season?" Frederick asked. "Summer? Autumn?"

"The social season, cloth-ears!" Bess was obviously happy to tutor Frederick. "From spring to midsummer, all the rich folk bring their daughters to town to marry them off, those rich enough or pretty enough to find a match. By this time of the summer, everyone is either married or bored out of their wits with parties and gossip, so they all go home. They let the harvest restore their pocketbooks, they spend the hunting season chasing all over the countryside after a pack of hounds, and as soon as Yuletide is past, they plan when to return to London and start all over again."

"But if their daughters have all been married off, why must they do it over?" Frederick asked.

Bess poked him. "Don't be simple. They must do something to keep busy, mustn't they? It's not as if they have floors to scrub. Geese fly south in the winter, and rich folk go to the country in the summer. That's just the way things are."

IN WHICH FREDERICK
LEARNS SOME HISTORY

Neither Frederick nor Bess had ever ridden in a private coach before, so the long jolting journey from the city to the wilds of Gloucestershire was a great adventure. Bess went inside the carriage with Mrs. Dutton and the maids. Mr. Kimball was riding on top of the coach with Frederick.

When at last the excitement of seeing the countryside had lost its novelty, Frederick began to find the sway and rattle of the carriage lulled him. To keep from falling asleep, Frederick peppered Mr. Kimball with questions.

"How long before we arrive?" Frederick asked. "How often do they change the teams of horses? Have you made this journey many times?"

"Not for hours," Mr. Kimball answered. "They change horses every twenty-five miles. In the past, I made the journey to Skeynes often. If the weather stays fair, it is a grand excursion. Skeynes is a noble house, the finest such property for miles in any direction. Lord Schofield did right to bring it back into good repair."

"Why was the place so neglected?" Frederick asked. "Because his lordship's brother died there?"

"Is that the gossip these days?" Mr. Kimball shook his head at such a notion. "No matter how great his sorrow, no true gentleman would let grief distract him from the welfare of his tenants and his property. No, Skeynes was left to itself for a time because it was cursed."

Frederick nearly fell off the coach. *"Cursed!"*

"Steady on," said Mr. Kimball. "The curse was broken. It took eleven wizards to remove the evil spell, and by the time they did, half the place was smashed to bits. You have no notion of the damage wizards can do when they set their minds to it."

Frederick couldn't help asking, "Worse than brownies and hobgoblins?"

"Brownies and hobgoblins? What have they to do with anything?" Mr. Kimball gave him a curious look but went on readily. "Far worse than that, I'm afraid. The curse was set upon the house by Sir Hilary Bedrick, one of the wickedest wizards who ever lived. He cast it the night he learned that the marquis had escaped the trap Sir Hilary had set for him. He meant to use Lord

Schofield the same way he'd used his older brother, Edward. By great good fortune, young Thomas saw through his scheme and was able to flee the country."

"Lord Schofield, you mean?" Frederick tried and failed utterly to imagine sturdy Lord Schofield as a young man.

"That's right. He had been studying magic with Sir Hilary. Right along, Sir Hilary fooled everyone. Just as he had sucked magic from Edward Schofield until he killed him, he was sucking magic from young Thomas. He went on stealing all he could, even after Lord Schofield escaped."

"How could he do that if Lord Schofield had run away from him?"

"To use their magic best, wizards must focus it. They put the magic into some object that looks quite ordinary. The focus can be anything, a ring or a walking stick or a lapel pin. Sir Hilary stole Thomas's focus and used it to siphon off his magic."

"But Sir Hilary was caught, wasn't he?" Frederick asked. "Lord Schofield got his focus back?"

"In the end, aye." Mr. Kimball smiled. "Lady Schofield helped. This was back in the days when he was courting her, of course. Talk of the town, they were. Fretted his lordship's mother so, she came all the way from Paris. His mother, Lady Sylvia that is, took a liking to our young Lady Schofield and gave her blessing to the match. Game as a pebble, that young lady."

Frederick wanted Kimball to get back to the point. "What about the curse? How was it broken?"

"I don't mean to leave bits out of the story," Mr. Kimball said, "but you ask too many questions. With Thomas safe out of the country, Lady Sylvia found wizards to break the curse, and lucky she did, for his lordship couldn't tell there was a curse on the place if it bit him on the nose. That was part of the curse, you see. He couldn't tell it was there. Even Lady Sylvia had difficulty sensing it, and she's a prime wizard herself."

"What was the curse?" Frederick demanded.

"Sir Hilary hated all the Schofields, and he wanted them to die. So that's what the curse was. Death to the Schofields. Lady Sylvia had married in, so she was not subject to the curse. But her surviving son was cursed to choke on Sir Hilary's hate."

Frederick could not help asking, "Why did he hate them so?"

"Magical ability runs in the Schofield family. He wanted their power for himself." All disapproval, Mr. Kimball shook his head. "A wicked man, no loss to anyone now he's dead."

Half afraid of the answer, Frederick made himself ask the question that leaped into his mind. "If Sir Hilary killed his brother, did Lord Schofield kill Sir Hilary?"

"That he didn't," said Mr. Kimball. "Sir Hilary had

the worst sort of criminals for friends. As he sowed, so did he reap. His accomplices killed him."

"Oh." Frederick felt relief that such a man was dead, and that no one he knew had been connected with the death. "But the curse outlived him?"

"The Royal College of Wizards shattered his curse to bits and swept it away forever," Mr. Kimball replied. "I promise you, no one would find me within fifty miles of the place if I thought otherwise. Sir Hilary is in his grave. The spells he cast can't harm anyone anymore."

Mr. Kimball's tales of magic made the journey seem short. For Frederick, who considered the view from atop the coach the finest in the world, it was all a thrilling adventure, until it began to rain.

Chilled to the bone, with every stitch he had on soaked, Frederick gave up feeling sorry for Bess, stuffed inside the coach with five other passengers, and felt sorry for himself instead.

"Pluck up," said Mr. Kimball, when Frederick was so weary and cold he was ready to fall off the lurching carriage into the muddy road. "We're nearly there. Only five miles to Skeynes from that crossroads we just passed. Be there in no time."

Nearly there in Mr. Kimball's terms was nothing like nearly there in Frederick's opinion, but at last, the carriage horses turned off the road to follow a freshly graveled driveway. The drive brought them through a park toward a house the size of a palace.

Even from a distance, even in the rain, the place was enough to astound Frederick. He thought he'd seen big houses in London. This house was many times larger than the one in Mayfair. It was almost a city all by itself. Skeynes was made of stone and glass. As the carriage approached, Frederick saw that a few of the windows already glowed with lamplight, although it wasn't yet dusk. Through the gloomy weather, Skeynes shone a welcome to the weary travelers.

Frederick couldn't make himself believe such a beautiful place had ever been cursed by anyone or anything. It looked like a royal palace out of the stories Vardle used to tell.

When at last they walked into the servants' hall at Skeynes, Frederick was so weary the stone floor he was dripping on seemed to float beneath his muddy feet.

"Take your boots off before you go one more step," Mr. Kimball ordered. "No need to track in more muck."

Dizzy with sleepiness, Frederick obeyed him. He found a place beside the fire and folded up in a dripping heap. Then, despite his discomfort, Frederick fell asleep before anyone even noticed he was there.

~

In the morning, Frederick felt much better. The fire had dried his clothes. The floor had already been scrubbed clean of yesterday's mud. But he was surprised and annoyed to discover someone had slipped half a dozen dried beans into his boots while he slept.

"It was probably one of the footmen," Bess told him when he complained at breakfast. "Remember the time you were sleeping in the laundry room and Jamie hid pease pudding in your breeches?"

"Oh, is that who did it?" Frederick promised himself he would stay well away from whichever footman Jamie turned out to be once he returned to the house in London. "Mr. Kimball didn't ask Jamie to come along to Skeynes with us, did he?"

"He didn't, so someone else must find you a tempting target. If you insist, I'll help you find out who did the dried beans. But after all, it was only beans. Throw them away and forget it. If you make a fuss, next time it will only be worse."

"I don't know about that. The footmen out here in the countryside may not be as inventive as the ones in town." Frederick sampled his bowl of porridge. "Oh, this is good."

Bess nodded. "My mother always told me there was nothing like the cream from the home farm at Skeynes, and she was right."

Frederick stared at the dried beans. "Or maybe it's just the wrong time of year for pease pudding."

"What is this on the floor? This is sour milk!" Mr. Grant's shouting made the kitchen rafters ring. "Who spilled milk and walked away without mopping it up? Am I among savages? Is this the way one makes cheese here in the howling wilderness? Has this kitchen never seen a scrub brush until now?"

"Hop it," Bess advised, "or we'll both be stuck here scrubbing."

IN WHICH FREDERICK
FEELS AT HOME

Skeynes was, Frederick discovered, the center of a whole new world. In addition to the great house and its stable block, there were outbuildings, a home farm, and what seemed like miles upon miles of gardens, fields, and forest.

Night and day, dozens of servants and farm laborers were busy at Skeynes. In London, Frederick had grown used to the divide between upper servants and lower servants. Now he discovered another divide, this one between London servants and local servants. All the London servants knew each other. All the local servants knew each other. But more than that, if the local servants weren't all blood relations, they behaved as if they were.

Bess had cousins aplenty among the local servants. The moment her work was done each day, they swept her off to catch up on family news and gossip. Frederick missed her. Strangely, he did not feel lonely. Although Skeynes might as well have been a foreign country, Frederick felt at home there from the very first morning.

In London Frederick's work had begun at daybreak, when the delivery wagons rumbled past and the cabs and carriages started the endless scurry of their day. At Skeynes, Frederick's work also began at daybreak, but there was not a sound of traffic anywhere. Not that it was quiet. If anything, Skeynes was noisier than London. For one thing, there were the birds. Frederick had seen birds in the city, sparrows mostly. In the countryside, there were more kinds of birds singing at once than Frederick had ever heard of before, more than he could count. There were also roosters, hens, and the occasional screaming peacock.

From Lord Schofield's bedchamber and dressing room, windows looked out over gardens, but Frederick had little chance to admire the view. He was too busy bringing the rooms into a proper state of cleanliness and order. With Lord and Lady Schofield expected any day, there was a tremendous amount of work to be done, from the attics and box rooms at the top of the house to the cellars beneath it.

The state of the cupboards in his lordship's dressing room was dreadful. Frederick spent his time clearing cobwebs and dusting. There would be no point in un-packing his lordship's wardrobe in a place that would dirty the clothing immediately. He took his time and did a thorough job. Frederick liked the sense of drowsy peace he found as he worked. Sometimes he felt that old sense of companionship, as if someone worked near him, just out of sight.

Before long, Frederick had Lord Schofield's dressing room looking as neat as a pin. The whole staff worked as hard as Frederick did and soon, in the matter of comfort and cleanliness, there was little to choose between the London house and Skeynes.

But in Lord Schofield's dressing room one morning, Frederick noticed soot in the grate of the fireplace. From the look of the debris he found, he suspected a bird was nesting up the chimney. Frederick wondered when the staff at Skeynes last had a proper chimney sweep in.

That evening at the long table in the servants' hall, Frederick remembered the soot. "Mr. Kimball, may I ask when the chimneys were last swept here?"

Mr. Kimball, seated at the far end of the table, was listening to Mrs. Dutton and did not hear the question. Frederick was too far away, seated with Bess and the local servants.

To his surprise, Rose, one of the few local maids Bess was not related to, slapped his wrist and burst out laughing. "Chimney sweeps! Don't remind us!" Still giggling, Rose turned to her sister Nancy. "Dreadful flirts, they were. How many did they send us?"

"Lost count after three," Nancy said. "Could have been an army of climbing boys up in those chimneys, with all the noise that lot made."

"Not surprised," muttered Bess. "I doubt either of you can count past three."

Fortunately, neither Rose nor Nancy heard Bess, but their giggling attracted Mr. Kimball's notice. "When were the chimneys last swept? It was last done thoroughly while Lord and Lady Schofield were away on their grand tour of the continent," Mr. Kimball said. "However, the household accounts show that there was a sweep here just a few months ago."

"Just the one." Rose giggled piercingly.

"Ah, but a good big one, he was," said Nancy. "Big enough to shift any amount of soot."

"Kept us dusting for days, he did," Rose agreed. "Thought my lungs would go black with it."

"Could have been a coal miner." Nancy giggled. "We won't want a fuss like that with Lord and Lady Schofield due here any day. Imagine them walking in on us with the house full of soot."

"We have plenty of time to prepare for their arrival," said Mr. Kimball. "I've had a letter from town. Lord and Lady Schofield find themselves unexpectedly detained.

Before you ask, I don't know for how long. They don't know themselves, I suspect. Time enough for another proper sweeping of the chimneys, though."

"They won't stay in town long," Bess murmured to Frederick. "Not with Mr. Grant here. They will miss his fancy cooking."

"I must arrange for a smaller sweep this time," Mr. Kimball said.

"Why smaller?" Frederick asked. "Wouldn't it be better to engage the biggest one you can find?"

"Strength is all very well in its way. But the smaller the sweep, the cleaner the chimneys, for a climbing boy can go higher than a grown man can, and is better by far at cleaning the narrow places."

"Mind you don't send up one *too* small," said Nancy, "or the spiders will eat him."

"Rose, if you can't stop giggling, you may be excused from the table." Mr. Kimball looked annoyed. "Your squeaking puts me off my food. You too, Nancy. The rest of you, mind your manners."

"Yes, Mr. Kimball. Thank you, Mr. Kimball."

Under her breath, Bess added, "The squeaks put me off too," but only Frederick heard her.

Very little put Frederick off his food. With Mr. Grant at Skeynes, the meals could not be faulted. Frederick thought the household did itself very well, despite its remote location. Some supplies came from London, but the eggs, cream, beef, bacon, and mutton were all from the home farm, and all of the best. After two weeks of it, Frederick's livery began to seem tight all over.

"You do look as if you've been stuffed," Bess observed, when he asked her about it. "I've grown a good bit myself. I asked Mrs. Dutton about it, and she sent me to see Hetty, the seamstress. But letting down a hem is much simpler than tailoring a jacket as fine as yours."

"Should I go see Hetty?" Frederick wondered. "What if she can't make it fit me again?"

"Try Mr. Kimball first. He likes your work. If Hetty can't help you, he may even send to London for new livery."

"Never," Frederick said. "What if they sack me? I was given my first position because I fit the livery. No one ever said anything about outgrowing it."

"Mr. Kimball wouldn't sack you for that, although there are some households that would. You can't help growing," Bess reminded him. "It's their own fault for feeding you."

"That's just what I'm afraid they'll think," Frederick said. "I've had enough of not eating to last me a lifetime."

∾☖∾

Hetty the seamstress welcomed Frederick to her work-room. She was a plump little woman in brown with a spotted scarf wrapped around her shoulders. The spots on the scarf and her quick sharp gestures made him think of a hen. "Mrs. Dutton told me you had Mr. Kimball's permission for my help, and I see you need it." She made him take his coat and breeches off.

Frederick sat on a stool in the corner while she in-spected the garments. "Do you think you can make it fit again?"

"Oh, yes. Plenty of room to let the seams back out." Hetty held up the coat to show him. "The tailor who fitted this for you knew his craft very well indeed. I've never seen such tiny stitches."

"There was no tailor." Frederick almost laughed at her mistake. "I only happened to fit the coat—it wasn't made for me. No fitting, I promise you."

"No?" Hetty smiled to herself. "You know best, of course. But I say, to sew a seam any finer, you'd have use magic."

Not for the first time, Frederick wondered how it was that the livery had come to fit him so exactly. Georgie, the previous orphan, had been a larger boy than Frederick. Had Billy Bly helped Frederick even then? Frederick wished he still had Billy Bly with him. There was so much he wanted to know.

"I saw it done once." Hetty had removed the lining

from the coat and was carefully picking out the stitch-
ing of the seams. "We had wizards here for the curse-
breaking, and afterward I saw one of them use magic
to mend a torn sleeve. Stitches so tiny he made, you
might look all day and never see the repairs."

Frederick drew his stool up a bit closer. "You were
here when this house was cursed?"

"Oh, yes. It wasn't so long ago, after all. The curse
was cast on the Schofield family, not on any of us."
Hetty's hands stilled as she thought back. "All the
same, we kept our distance. *Such evil may cast shadows,*
the wizards told us, so we took care."

"Were you here when the curse was broken?"

Hetty threaded her needle and began to sew up the
seams again. "I said we kept our distance. We were
down in the village. Dreadful it was, though. Even
from there."

"What was it like?" Frederick asked.

"Like a summer storm, all darkness and lightning.
We saw flashes of light all the way down in the village.
What we heard of it was like thunder." Hetty looked up
from her needlework. "One of the wizards, young Mr.
Pickering with the torn sleeve, had a weakness for my
mother's pastry. He told us stories afterward. He said
at times it was like something squeaking, something
between a mouse and a bat. Young ears are better than
old, so he heard it better than the old wizards could,

it was that high-pitched. Sometimes though, the worst times, it was shrieking. It was the shrieks that broke the windows, he told us."

"Get along with you," said Frederick. "How can a shriek break a window? A shriek is just a loud noise."

"Magic," Hetty replied. "If you ever hear the like, you run, understand? Don't look around to see where it comes from. Just run."

"Now you're making fun of me because I'm from the city," Frederick said.

"Cross my heart, it's true, every word," said Hetty. "It was worst in the room his lordship sleeps in. That's what the young wizard told us. He wasn't mocking us, I swear it. He had too much fondness for pastry to risk losing Mother's goodwill."

"Shrieking." Frederick shook his head. "Squeaks and shrieks. You were better off with thunder and lightning, Hetty."

"I hope you never find out different." Hetty set the coat aside. "Now, let's see about your breeches."

IN WHICH FREDERICK LEARNS
WHAT HE HAS BEEN MISSING

The morning after Hetty finished the alterations, Frederick found six dried peas in his boots. His first impulse was to look for a snickering footman. When he found no sign of any, he went to Bess for advice.

"So it happened again, did it?" Bess smiled, but somehow Frederick didn't mind it when she showed her amusement at his actions. Bess was different. When she snickered, he did too.

"This time"—Frederick held out his hand to show her—"it was peas."

"I'm to fetch Mr. Grant a dozen fresh eggs," said Bess. "Come along with me."

As they made their way down the lane to the home farm, Frederick thought about the peas and beans. Not much to be fretting over, a few peas and beans. It made him miss Billy Bly all over again. Peas and beans were harmless enough, after all. "Do you still think I should forget about it?"

"I know you should forget it." Bess swung her basket to emphasize her words. "Take no notice. Unless you *want* whoever it is to go to more trouble and make a greater mess."

"Who do you think did it?" Frederick persisted. "Do you think it was the same one who spilled milk in the kitchen and left it to go sour?"

"Oh, I don't know." Bess tugged at his sleeve. "If you don't pick your feet up a bit more, I'll be late."

"I can't go any faster, not without stepping in a cowpat." They had come to a particularly smelly bit of footing. Frederick felt he was completely entitled to choose his way with care. "Let alone the sheep droppings."

Bess didn't slacken her pace. "Oh, don't be such a dandy. You clean your own boots every night, no matter what. Just this one time, they will need it. That won't kill you. Come on!"

As he was cleaning the manure off his boots later, Frederick remembered the exchange with Bess. He wondered what he was going to find in his boots the next morning. Better than simply ignoring whatever it was, Frederick thought, would be making it more difficult for the other servants to meddle with his things. Frederick went in search of Mr. Kimball to ask for permission to sleep elsewhere in the future.

"The servants at Skeynes are quartered in the attic," said Mr. Kimball. "Where else would you wish to sleep?"

"Wouldn't I be more use to his lordship if I were close at hand?" Frederick asked. "Somewhere near his bedchamber? I can make up a bed for myself in a corner of his dressing room."

Mr. Kimball thought it over. "Very well. You may sleep in Lord Schofield's dressing room, provided you keep an eye on the fire in his lordship's bedchamber. You wouldn't credit how it can smoke at times. There must be something wrong with that flue."

Lord Schofield's dressing room was just off the room where Lord Schofield usually slept. With luck, Frederick thought, he might learn a bit more about the curse on that bedchamber. "I keep seeing fresh soot in the grate of the dressing room fireplace in the mornings. I think there must be a bird's nest somewhere up in the flue."

"Possibly." Mr. Kimball frowned. "I'll send for the sweep at once."

As good as his word, Mr. Kimball had the chimney sweep in the very next day. As the maids had predicted, the soot was dreadful. Nothing of interest was found anywhere in the chimneys, not so much as a bird's feather, nothing to explain any problems with the flues. By the end of the week, the last of the general household soot had been dusted away and cleanliness restored. But by Sunday morning, Frederick found fresh flecks of black in the dressing room fireplace.

The first chance he had, Frederick showed Mr. Kimball the soot.

"Looks like soot, you're right about that," said Mr. Kimball. "No chance anyone used that fireplace without you noticing?"

"No chance at all. You don't suppose it has something to do with the curse, do you?" Frederick asked.

Mr. Kimball looked offended. "I do not! Nothing of the sort. Obviously there's something nesting up there somewhere, a bird or a squirrel, something the sweep just didn't notice."

The next night that he slept in Lord Schofield's dressing room, Frederick woke in the dark. His eyes told him nothing, but he distinctly heard the sound of dry leaves rustling. At first Frederick, still half dreaming, took it for granted. When he could, he always slept with a window open. After a few moments, however, he woke up enough to remember that the little window in the dressing room didn't open. Whatever the sound was, it didn't come from outdoors.

Frederick pushed up on one elbow, staring around despite the darkness. He strained his ears, grateful he heard no squeaking of any kind.

No squeaking, but just beside him, a soft deep voice murmured, "Warn his nibs, young Frederick. There's something in the chimney, something I can't catch. It won't hurt me, but if it can, it might hurt you. For certain sure, it will try to hurt his lordship."

"Billy Bly?" Frederick reached out toward the voice, feeling nothing but air. "You're *here*?"

"You noticed. I was starting to think you never would." The deep voice came from the far end of the bed as Billy Bly tugged at Frederick's blanket to wrap it more snugly around Frederick's feet. "Of course I'm here. Who else would it be?"

With all his heart, Frederick wished for a light. "You're really here!"

"Aye. You were flitting, so I flitted too."

"But Lord Schofield banished you."

"From his house, as he had every right to do," Billy Bly agreed. "Not from every house. His nibs never mentioned this place."

"You know what he meant," Frederick said.

"Did I? I know what he *said*." Billy Bly chuckled, a dry sound like leaves rustling. "At best, magic only does what you say. No guarantee it ever does what you want. What his nibs meant doesn't enter into it, not unless he said it just exactly so."

"When did you come? How long have you been here?"

"As long as you have." The voice in the dark sounded cross. "You're not half thick, lad. You didn't notice my message? I had a job finding dried beans and dried peas at this time of year, I can tell you."

Frederick felt foolish for missing the significance of the peas and beans. "I thought one of the other servants did that just to be a nuisance."

"I did it so you would know I was watching out for you. I don't fancy letting any of the other servants see me." Under his breath, Billy Bly added, "Rubies to radishes they would tattle to that butler about me."

Frederick let the familiar sense of companionship he associated with Billy Bly's presence wash over him. It felt like a good meal when he was hungry. It felt like the warmth of a well-laid fire on a cold wet night. It felt like coming home. Frederick couldn' eep the words back. "I missed you. I don't want Lord Schofield to banish you again."

Billy Bly sounded somewhat embarrassed. "And I missed you too, lad. But there's no help for it this time. You must warn his nibs-ship not to come here. The wizard is too proud of his family home to stay away, but all the while he is here, he's in deadly peril."

"Is it the curse?" Frederick asked. "Is that what you found in the chimney?"

"I found something. I can't tell you much about curses," said Billy Bly. "They don't work on us brownies the way they do on you mortals. I've tried talking with it, but I can't get a word out of the thing. Whether it can't answer me or whether it won't, I couldn't say. What I do know is, that thing is bad. It looks nasty. It feels nasty. It even tastes nasty. It's huge, but it moves too fast for me to catch. When I do get a grip on it, bits of it come away in my hands. Fair makes my skin crawl, but it doesn't slow the thing down a jot."

Frederick asked, "Is it some kind of animal, then?"

Billy Bly sounded very grave. "It's no animal. Not a snake, though it looks like one. It stinks of malice. Sometimes it looks like a bit of rope. Sometimes it's as thick as your neck, but sometimes it's long and thin. Depends on where it is hiding in the chimney. Some places are too small even for me to reach."

Frederick kicked his legs free of the blanket. "Let me help you catch it. What if we had a net? Do you think a net would work?"

"Stay." Billy Bly sounded stern. "I didn't come to rouse you. I don't want the whole house on end. Bad enough I spilled a pint of milk when I was chasing it out of the kitchen."

"That was you?" Frederick asked. "Mr. Grant was in a dreadful strop about that spilled milk."

"Sun was up before I had a chance to return to the kitchen. By then the maids were stirring. I dared not stay to clean it up. His nibs won't be happy to learn

I am here, for things do seem to happen when I'm around. Fragile keepsakes fall and smash. It's the way of things. But learn I'm here he must, lad. You must give him a message."

"No!" Frederick tried to rise.

"Yes!" Billy Bly twisted the blanket so tight around his legs that Frederick could hardly wriggle. "Do it however you please, but don't let Thomas Schofield come here without warning him of the danger."

"How am I going to tell his lordship about the thing in the chimney without letting him know you're here?" Frederick asked. "He's sure to send you away again."

"Let him."

Frederick's throat grew so tight he could hardly get words out. "I won't. I can't."

"All the same, you must warn him."

Frederick clutched his head in despair. "*Dear Lord Schofield. Don't come here. There's a bit of rope in the chimney. Your obedient servant, Frederick Lincoln.* Is that what you want me to tell him?"

"Seems to me that would do the trick nicely. But suit yourself," said Billy Bly when Frederick emitted a fizzing sound of disagreement. "If you can't think how to put it, ask that young red-haired maid of yours. She knows how to do things properly. Don't let the grass grow between your toes while you fret over what to do.

Send a message and send it soon. Soon! Better to do it badly than leave the task undone."

With one last tug at the blanket to tuck Frederick in, Billy Bly departed. Frederick found himself alone in a perfectly silent room. Nothing rustled but Frederick, fighting to escape his bedding.

Once he was free, Frederick made himself lie quiet and still, but he did not sleep for a long time. Instead he stared up into the dark, ears straining for the sound of anything, anything at all, lurking in the chimney. Young ears are better than old, Hetty had told him. Frederick was glad of it. It would be terrible to be old and deaf and never know if something full of malice, something that could look like a snake or a bit of rope, was coming after him in the dark.

Houses make noise at night, Frederick discovered. Each time he began to drift to sleep, a distant window would rattle or a nearby floorboard would creak. He started awake again and again, frightened. The sense of peace and comfort that usually accompanied the rustling noise he associated with Billy Bly was gone. Instead, Frederick found himself on watch in the night, waiting for danger that never came.

In the morning, a message arrived express for Mr. Kimball. Within minutes, the whole staff had the news:

Lord and Lady Schofield were to arrive that very day. Everyone worked with particular zeal to bring Skeynes to a peak of beauty and comfort. Frederick was finished with his duties by midday, so he went to find Bess.

The moment Bess laid eyes on him, she felt his forehead. "Frederick, what's wrong? Are you running a fever? You look dreadful. Are you sickening for something?"

"No. I need your help." Frederick urged Bess out of the servants' hall and down the steps toward the still room. "You mustn't tell anyone. Not anyone. Promise!"

"What's happened? Are you sure you're not sick?" Bess let Frederick chivy her until they were out of sight of the other servants, then dug in her heels and refused to go another step. "Are you in trouble? Whatever it is, I can't promise anything until you tell me what you want."

"I'm not in trouble." Frederick took a good look at Bess and decided to risk complete honesty. "Promise you won't tell."

"I can only promise to use my wits." Bess put her hands on her hips and glared at him. "Tell me."

The way Bess's eyes flashed, Frederick knew it was no use trying to swear her to secrecy first. Trusting to her good sense, he told her everything he knew.

Bess was silent for long moments after Frederick

finished speaking. When she spoke at last, she was frowning so fiercely, Frederick thought for a moment she might be angry with him. "You must warn his lordship. He and Lady Schofield are to arrive today, so there's no time to send a message."

Frederick had worked that much out for himself. "I could try to stop the carriage, but if I wait until they pull up at the door, he might ignore me and go straight in before I can get his attention."

"You're right." Bess's face brightened. "Do you know the gatehouse, just off the main road? The carriage slows down there to make the turn. If you wait at the gatehouse, you can warn his lordship before the carriage comes near the house."

Frederick started for the door. "Tell me how to find it. Do I just keep on down the lane until I reach the main road?"

"Yes, it's easy—but I'll show you the way. Just wait half a moment—I must put on my bonnet." Bess whisked off.

Frederick did not wait. He knew he risked losing his position, abandoning his duties without permission to lie in wait for his lordship's carriage. It would never do for Bess to get the sack because she helped him do it. He legged it out the door and across the stable yard.

Not five hundred yards down the lane, Bess caught

up with him, bonnet crooked and face scarlet with suppressed rage. "Traitor!"

Frederick didn't slow down. "No sense in both of us risking the sack. Go back."

Despite her skirts, Bess matched him stride for stride with no difficulty. "Not a chance."

Sometimes only walking fast, but sometimes running, they hurried down the graveled lane together. On either hand grew tall hedges full of birds and blossoms. Frederick ignored the beauty of the day. He had a grim message to deliver.

IN WHICH FREDERICK
DELIVERS A MESSAGE

Where the lane met the main road was the gatehouse Bess had spoken of. Although the gatehouse was old, it was new to Frederick. Intent on his first glimpse of Skeynes, he had been looking the other way when the coach arrived. To Frederick, it looked like a cottage made out of the forest itself. Moss covered the steep roof. Ivy grew over the walls so thick, the gatehouse was easy to miss.

Bess rapped at the door until Stoke the gatekeeper emerged. He moved so slowly, Frederick half expected the old man to have patches of moss himself.

"What's the trouble, young ones?" The gatekeeper, once he finally joined them, had a voice as slow as his steps. He took his time sizing them up. "You two look all of a rumple. What's wrong?"

Bess told Stoke who they were. "We have a message

we *must* give to his lordship as soon as possible."

Frederick added, "It's important."

"Is it, now?" The gatekeeper scratched at his chin whiskers. "Unaccountable flighty his young lordship has always been, but word has come he means to arrive today. Settle down on the bench here. We will watch for him together."

Bess accepted the offer with thanks. Frederick sat down beside her and looked around. The stone wall was in good repair, but there was no sign whatever of a gate. "What good is a gatehouse without a gate?" he muttered to Bess.

Despite his years, there seemed nothing whatever wrong with Stoke's hearing. "There's gates and then there's gates, youngster. If you mean a big door you can lock, there was a gate here once, but that was long ago. It's gone to ruins now. They nearly let this gate-house go to ruins too, but his lordship had them mend my roof when he mended the great house, after the wizards finished their house cleaning."

Frederick sat up straight. "You were here when the curse was broken?" Stoke certainly looked as if he'd been there since Noah's flood.

"That I was, youngster." Stoke scratched at his chin again. "Some say wizards only play tricks on those they claim to help. I know better. Those wizards earned every penny of their wages."

Frederick could hardly keep his seat. "What did they do? What was it like?"

"It was like spring-cleaning in a madhouse. I kept my distance, but there were flashes like lightning over the trees there. When morning came at last, we had rain like it would never stop. You wouldn't believe me now, if I told you how this roof leaked. Fair washed me away. Now for you and the lass. Must be something dreadful important to bring the pair of you out from the great house and away from your duties for so long, all lest you miss his lordship."

Frederick nodded. His conscience pained him enough as it was. He didn't want to add lying to his misdeeds. Stoke didn't seem like the sort of person one could tell lies to. So Frederick held his peace. When he didn't speak and Bess didn't either, Stoke let the silence grow for several minutes.

At last, the old man turned to Bess. "With that ginger hair of yours, you have a look about you, lass, and a look I think I know. Is your mother Mary Briggs?"

"She was before she wed my father," Bess answered. "She's Mistress Mary Parker now."

Stoke was delighted. "I thought I knew the look of you. Your mother was maid here at Skeynes and met your father when she went off to London with the old lord and lady."

"Yes. Papa was a footman in the London household," Bess said. "He is Lord Ravelston's butler now."

"Are you the only child?" Stoke asked.

"Oh, no. I have two sisters and a brother," said Bess. "I'm young to be one of the maids brought to Skeynes, but Mama wanted me to know her family here. I have an aunt working in the dairy at the home farm. Another year and Clarence, that's my brother, ought to find a position in the London household as well."

Frederick looked at Bess with wonder. "Is that why you were so happy to be sent off to the country? I didn't know your mother was so good at arranging things."

Bess looked pleased with herself. "I would have told you all about it, if you had seemed even a little interested. It is because you don't have family of your own. You never think to ask."

Stoke beamed his approval. "Good for you, lass, for keeping your tongue still. Plenty of folk clack far too freely, to folk they think they know, and worse, to strangers."

"You may always clack to me, Bess," Frederick said. "You know that, don't you?"

Bess laughed at him. "You must clack to me first."

"I do," said Frederick, remembering how he had trusted her with news of Billy Bly's return almost without a second thought. "I clack to you more than to anyone else."

"And that's good for you, lad," Stoke observed. "Choose a friend who knows how to keep a confidence. You won't regret it."

The three of them chatted companionably until the day drew to a close. Stoke, happy to play the host, shared his porridge with them. After the dishes had been washed up, they sat on the bench again, in silence this time, just enjoying the peace of the long summer twilight.

Frederick lifted his head to listen as the breeze brought them a scrap of new sound from the distance. It was little more than a rattle of wheels and the ring of harness, the sound of a carriage driven at a good, steady speed.

At Frederick's reaction, Stoke nodded. "You hear it too?"

"A carriage?" Bess asked. "Is it his lordship's?"

"That we won't know until we see them," Stoke replied. "Likely it is, though. It's a carriage drawn by four horses. No cart horses, neither. Proper high-bred 'uns."

The three of them strained eyes and ears in the dusk. Bit by bit, the sounds of a carriage approaching grew louder and more complex. There was a steady thud of hooves, a squeaking of carriage springs, a bright chime of metal on metal as harness fittings rattled and shook.

"Not in a hurry, I'd say," said Stoke as he moved out into the roadway. "But it's a spanking trot for any team and a cracking good rate for a team at the end of a long day."

Frederick felt as if his breeches itched, he was so eager to warn Lord Schofield of his danger. He and Bess flanked Stoke. When the carriage finally came into view around the nearest turn, all three of them waved their arms and shouted.

It was Lord Schofield's carriage, right enough. The four horses went from a steady trot to a walk under the command of the driver, Lord Schofield himself. As the carriage slowed, Lord Schofield gave the reins to his coachman.

"Walk them, Foster." Lord Schofield clambered down from his perch. He spoke a few words into the open window of the carriage, then hurried over to join them. "What is it, Stoke? Trouble?"

"That's as may be, your lordship," Stoke replied, jerking a thumb in Frederick's direction. "There's a message for you."

Now that the moment had finally come, Frederick couldn't think of a thing to say that didn't begin with the dangerous words *Billy Bly,* so he simply stared at Lord Schofield without speaking. He knew Stoke was looking on with interest. He felt Bess right beside him, all silent encouragement. Yet he did not know what to say.

"Oh, it's you, is it?" Lord Schofield took off his top hat and wiped his forehead with his handkerchief. "Taken a vow of silence?"

Here was someone Frederick knew he dared not lie to. He only wanted to tell the truth, nothing but the truth. Yet not the whole truth. Frederick braced himself and began. "The curse has returned, my lord. You mustn't come back. You're in great danger if you do."

Lord Schofield grew quite still. For a moment, he might have been a statue, he was so motionless. Only his eyes burned into Frederick. When he spoke, his lips scarcely moved. His voice was so deep, it seemed to rumble in his chest. "Go on."

"That's all, my lord." Frederick was caught in Lord Schofield's gaze. He could not look away. His childish fear of having his bones ground to powder by the wizard did not seem so silly after all.

"No, it isn't." Lord Schofield's tone was gentle but his eyes were relentless. "Go on."

Before Frederick could speak, the carriage door opened. Piers emerged and helped Lady Schofield descend. As she made her way to join them, Frederick saw by her thick figure and slow gait that she was expecting a child. Frederick found her presence comforting. Surely his lordship would not do anything too dreadful to him in front of his young wife?

Bess poked Frederick in the ribs. It took him a moment to understand why. Only when she dropped a curtsy to her ladyship did Frederick remember to make a bow to Lady Schofield himself.

"What's the trouble, Thomas?" Lady Schofield looked tired and pale. "Is something wrong?"

"What an excellent question. Out with it, Frederick," said Lord Schofield. "What have you done?"

"Me? I never," Frederick protested.

Lord Schofield was stern. "Speak now, young Frederick, or forever hold your peace."

Frederick stammered a little as he began. He wanted to leave all mention of Billy Bly out of his account. But that omission made it hard to organize his thoughts properly. As he went on, bit by bit, he grew more forceful. "I—that is, with Mr. Kimball's permission, your lordship—I sleep in your dressing room. Things aren't right. There's something in the chimney, sir, something not natural. They've had the sweeps in again and again, but something's amiss up there. I know you had eleven wizards in to break the curse on your house, but they said it could grow back. It has."

"Has it?" Lord Schofield turned to his wife. "Kate, given your condition, I assume you won't mind waiting here with Piers. You will have Stoke and the maid to look after you while I investigate this."

"You may assume nothing of the sort." Lady Schofield raised a hand to stop her husband before he could protest. "I mind waiting very much, here or anywhere else."

"You will be perfectly safe and comfortable here. Piers will be with you." Lord Schofield kept his stern gaze on Frederick. "The lad comes with me."

Lady Schofield answered, "I only mind because you intend to go off without me."

"Oh, don't worry about that. If something goes wrong, I will return. Piers and I shall whisk you off to Gloucester," Lord Schofield replied.

"You will do no such thing." Lady Schofield was all patience. "We have discussed this more than once, Thomas. There are situations when it is best we stay together. I thought we had agreed."

Frederick could not quite understand why she was still holding up her left hand before Lord Schofield's face, but Lord Schofield seemed to feel she had made a good point. He took her gloved hand and kissed it just where her wedding ring would be.

"Oh, very well. But if you insist I focus on the work before us, you must stay close to me. Now. First things first. Fetch a light, Stoke. Piers, keep your eyes open."

It took time, but Stoke eventually emerged from the gatehouse bearing a lantern. The golden light it cast made Frederick notice how the long dusk had finally turned into evening.

"Excellent. Hold it for me just there." Lord Schofield positioned Stoke and the lantern carefully, then handed his gloves to his wife.

As Lady Schofield and the servants all looked on in silence, Lord Schofield used the index finger of his right hand to trace a circle in the dust of the lane. As he worked, he murmured to himself, words Frederick did not understand. When the circle had been marked here and there with seemingly random lines, Lord Schofield straightened to his full height. Muttering all the while, he made three quick hand gestures, as if he were giving someone directions. At last, he bent over and studied the circle intently.

Frederick saw nothing to account for Lord Schofield's interest. It was just a circle in the dirt.

"Bearing in mind that I never perceived the original curse, nothing I do can establish absolutely the presence *or* absence of an evil spell. Still, it looks clear to me." Lord Schofield sighed and dusted his hands. Lady Schofield gave him back his gloves. Frowning, he drew them on. "I would be a great deal happier if you would permit me to take you somewhere else for the night, Kate."

"It looks clear to you," said Lady Schofield. "Meaning, you detect nothing to suggest there's any danger?"

"Not so much as a shimmer that shouldn't be there. But that's only my perception. Ought we to call in reinforcements, would you say?"

"More people, when we have come all this way to find a bit of peace and quiet?" Lady Schofield smiled fondly at him. "If you think it is safe, take me home, Thomas."

As he drew his wife close, Lord Schofield's expression was soppiness personified. "Oh, Kate."

Disgusted by the sentimentality, Frederick had to look away.

"I promise, at the sound of the first shriek, I will insist you drive us both back to London," said Lady Schofield.

"That's all very well," grumbled Lord Schofield. "What if I'm the one shrieking?"

"In all the time I have known you, I have never heard you shriek." Lady Schofield thought it over. "It's more of a roaring sound."

"Piers, bring the lantern." Lord Schofield offered his arm to Lady Schofield and the pair of them strolled up the drive toward the house. "I never roar. And after all, you haven't known me so long as all that."

Frederick, vexed at their air of being out for a twilight stroll, followed Piers and the lantern, with Bess still at his elbow. Foster, now driving the carriage and letting the horses amble slowly along, brought up the rear. Stoke waved them off and went back inside the gatehouse.

"It's been years since we met," Lady Schofield said.

"If ever you were going to shriek, surely I would have heard you do so by now."

"You have a point," Lord Schofield said. "Still, you never know. I might shriek at any moment."

"It will be more of a roar," Lady Schofield predicted. "Not that you couldn't shriek beautifully if you took a notion to do so, my dear."

After a hundred yards of this, Frederick dropped back far enough that he did not have to listen to any more of their foolish chatter. He didn't know how Piers kept from retching.

Night had fallen by the time they reached the house.

"Not the best light to admire it by," said Lord Schofield to his wife, "but welcome to your new home just the same, Kate. Custom now demands I carry you over the threshold."

"Common sense forbids it," Lady Schofield replied firmly.

"That lets me out, then." So saying, Lord Schofield swept Lady Schofield up in his arms and carried her bodily up the steps. Alarmed, Frederick brought up the rear, ready to brace his employer if he lost his balance under the burden.

Mr. Kimball must have been watching their approach, for the front door swung open just as Lord Schofield reached the top step. Lord Schofield's hat fell off but he did not hesitate. He carried his wife over the threshold and put her back on her feet in the front hall. Bess helped her tidy the disarray his lordship's grip caused to Lady Schofield's gown.

Frederick picked up the top hat and brushed it off carefully. From his place at the threshold Frederick saw the whole front hall was lined with servants, all standing at attention.

"Welcome to Skeynes, my lady," Mr. Kimball said, bowing. "Welcome home, my lord."

Graciously, with a smile and a word for each of them, Lady Schofield greeted her staff, from Mr. Kimball down to the youngest maids. At her heels, Lord Schofield beamed with pride. Piers fell into line with the other servants. Frederick stood between Piers and Bess.

At last the welcome was over. Lady Schofield turned to Lord Schofield. "Are we ready to continue the investigation?"

Despite all the nonsense she had spouted about shrieks and roars, Frederick decided Lady Schofield might be more sensible than Lord Schofield after all.

"Why not?" Lord Schofield was still beaming at her as they climbed the front stair. Servants were supposed to use the back stairs, but Frederick followed them, making it look as much as possible as if he were entrusted with important luggage, even though all he carried was Lord Schofield's top hat.

Frederick was surprised when, despite the warning they'd been given, Lord and Lady Schofield walked boldly into the dressing room off his lordship's bedchamber. "The curse!" he reminded them as he followed.

Lord Schofield didn't glance up from where he was marking a circle on the floor, this time with a bit of chalk from his pocket. "No sign of one yet. No sign of anything."

"I like this house." Lady Schofield was smiling as she looked around. "So peaceful."

Frederick checked the dressing room over as he put the top hat away. No dried peas, nor any other sign of Billy Bly's visit. No soot in the fireplace. The place was trim and spotless.

Lord Schofield muttered and gestured his way through his spell once more, then sighed, "Safe!" and rubbed the chalk marks out with his pocket handkerchief. "To be perfectly methodical about it, I'll do a great cleansing ritual, but that can wait for morning."

"Good." Lady Schofield took his hands in hers. "We're both worn out."

Frederick left the young couple gazing into each other's eyes. Revolting, the way otherwise sensible people could carry on, he decided. Something to do with being married, no doubt. Perhaps it damaged the brain.

IN WHICH FREDERICK SEES
MORE THAN HE SHOULD

In the morning, Frederick was relieved to discover Lord Schofield was back in his right mind. The whole time Piers shaved him, he seemed to be thinking deeply. When he was finally dressed, Lord Schofield dismissed Piers and fixed Frederick with a glance. "It is just the two of us here now, so you may speak freely. Don't be embarrassed that you cried wolf. Everyone makes the occasional mistake. What gave you the idea the curse has returned?"

"It *has,* my lord." Frederick felt as if Lord Schofield could see clear through him like a pane of glass.

"I knew the rumors would fly the moment Skeynes was lived in again. I didn't think you'd be the one to spread them." Lord Schofield turned away from Frederick and adjusted his cravat in the looking glass.

Frederick knew he should make some excuse to

leave his employer's presence, but he couldn't stop himself from speaking. "Can't you believe me?"

Lord Schofield moved so he was watching Frederick in the mirror. "Tell me why I should. Who told you the curse was back?"

Frederick wished to answer honestly, yet he could not bring himself to betray the presence of Billy Bly. Even if he told Lord Schofield straight out, there was the chance the wizard would refuse to believe him. The silence stretched until Lord Schofield broke it.

"You won't give me your gossip's name. I admire your determination to keep them from my wrath. I won't have Lady Schofield troubled by these rumors, understand?"

Frederick nodded.

"Very well." Lord Schofield looked thoughtful. "Time for the cleansing spell, I think. Bring me a broom, a pint of ale, a pint of water you've drawn from the well yourself, a pound of salt, a lot of rosemary, and a handful of feathers, any sort, so long as they are clean."

It took the best part of an hour for Frederick to fetch everything. Then, despite the fine weather, Lord Schofield ordered Frederick to kindle a fire in the dressing room hearth. The flue drew properly, smoke rising just as it should, without drifting back into the dressing room.

"That's interesting," Lord Schofield said, peering

into the depths of the fireplace to watch the smoke going up.

While Frederick had been carrying out all his instructions, Lord Schofield had assembled his magical implements. There was now an embroidered cloth on the shaving stand where the set of razors was normally kept. On the cloth lay an array of objects, some as familiar as a battered-looking kitchen knife, some too strange for Frederick to put names to.

Lord Schofield tossed a pinch of salt on the flames. "Hand me the broom. Now, stand in the doorway and don't let anyone else in, no matter what."

"Not even Lady Schofield?" Frederick took up the position Lord Schofield indicated.

"At this hour? She will still be sleeping. But no, just this once, not even Kate. Now be quiet."

Slowly, far more slowly and far less thoroughly than Frederick would have done it, Lord Schofield swept the entire dressing room. With every stroke of the broom, he muttered to himself. The sweepings, what few there were, went on the fire. Then out came the chalk again. This time it was not a circle Lord Schofield drew on the floor, but a triangle. He made marks around the outside of the triangle, but if they were words, they were written in no alphabet Frederick had ever seen before.

The salt, Lord Schofield sprinkled in a ring around

the triangle. The rosemary and the feathers were distributed at irregular intervals within the ring. Lord Schofield put a crystal dish in the center of the triangle and poured in as much well water as it would hold. All the while, his muttering went on, a soft chant Frederick did not understand, even though it sounded half familiar.

At first, Frederick worried that Lord Schofield would catch some hint that Billy Bly was in the house. But soon that concern faded. The fire on the hearth made the room seem uncomfortably warm.

Frederick yawned. Even though he and Lord Schofield were the only ones in it, the room felt crowded. Frederick yawned a second time. Trying to wake himself up fully, Frederick squeezed his eyes shut hard, opened them, and looked again at the scene before him. The ring of salt, it seemed to Frederick, was whiter than it had been. The crystal dish of water seemed not as full. Lord Schofield kept on chanting.

The rosemary drooped and wilted. The feathers looked exactly as they had when Frederick collected them from the first hen to cross his path in the farmyard. The crackling of the fire made Frederick feel drowsy. If anything, the room had grown more stuffy than before. At last, Lord Schofield put his hands together over his heart and fell silent.

Almost overwhelmed by the warmth of the fire in

the stuffy room, Frederick yawned a third time.

Lord Schofield glared at Frederick as he took up the broom and swept the whole arrangement into a heap in the center of the triangle. He disposed of the mess in the fireplace and added a few sticks of firewood to help the blaze along. Then Lord Schofield used the water in the crystal dish to wash the floor clean. At last, when the final traces of the ritual had been tidied away, he spoke. "Stop yawning, you infernal nuisance, and make yourself useful. Hand me that tankard of ale."

Frederick obeyed. Lord Schofield leaned on the broom as he drank the ale in hasty gulps. He smacked his lips and sighed. "That's better."

"Salt doesn't burn." Frederick stared at the blaze in the hearth. He glimpsed strange colors in the flames. "Is that salt burning because you made it go whiter?"

The empty tankard hit the floor with a clank. Frederick felt the weight of Lord Schofield's hand heavy on his shoulder. "What do you see?"

For a moment, Frederick could not utter a word. He was held fast in Lord Schofield's piercing gaze. He was filled with fear that his employer saw right through him to the truth about Billy Bly.

Lord Schofield gave Frederick's shoulder a gentle shake. "Well? Speak up. What do you see in the flames?"

Frederick looked back at the hearth. If he didn't

look at Lord Schofield, he could speak normally. If he didn't let himself think about Billy Bly, he could tell the truth about everything else. "The ring of salt looked whiter when you were mumbling, that's all. Is that why the fire turns green and blue now and then?"

"No." Lord Schofield released him and took a step or two away. When at last he answered Frederick's question, he seemed absentminded, as if he were thinking of something else entirely. "The cleansing spell absorbs all manner of impurities. It makes people sleepy too. I don't know why."

"But why does the fire burn green and blue?" Frederick persisted.

"The salt changes its nature when it takes the impurities in, just as the nature of the impurity is changed by the spell. That's what burns green and blue, the residue."

Frederick dared to glance back at his employer. "There were impurities, then?"

"A great many of them," Lord Schofield agreed. "More than enough to account for the sinister signs you reported. Don't speak of this to Lady Schofield. Given her condition, I won't have her troubled."

"What condition?" Frederick picked up the discarded tankard. "She seemed perfectly well last night."

Lord Schofield handed him the broom. "Take this back to the kitchen and tell someone to thump you on the head with it until your eyes function properly. Lady Schofield, as everyone else has noticed, is expecting a child."

"Oh, that." Relieved, Frederick accepted the broom. "I thought you said she had a condition."

"That *is* her condition," Lord Schofield retorted, "and I won't have her fretting herself over gossip and rumors. The physicians agreed. The quiet of the countryside, and more to the point, the complete absence of any members of her family, will do her good. Now that she's safely here, I mean for her to have peace and quiet. She shall, if it means I have to strangle every person I see."

He knew it was never wise to presume on Lord Schofield's good nature, but Frederick couldn't keep silent any longer. "That's *your* condition, sir."

"Out of my sight, saucebox, or I shall begin the strangling with you," said Lord Schofield. "If you weren't so clever about tying a cravat, I would turn you off without a reference."

"You would, too." Frederick put his whole heart into looking as sad as possible, no easy task, for he felt the smile he was trying to hide quirking at the corners of his mouth.

"I would!" Lord Schofield assured him. "Now go!"

That very day, at dinner in the servants' hall, Mr. Kimball gave the staff the official announcement. "Having taken advice from the finest physicians and manmidwives in London, it was agreed the peace of the countryside would be best for Lady Schofield's confinement. With God's grace, she will give birth to his lordship's first child here at Skeynes sometime in November."

The servants had known of the pregnancy from their first look at Lady Schofield. All the same, they rejoiced at the announcement, for it meant they could speak openly of the expected event. Grant raised his glass. "If it is a boy, his lordship will stand us all champagne."

"Never mind a few sips of champagne," Mr. Kimball said. "If it is a boy, there will be brown ale enough for young Frederick here to swim in."

Frederick didn't know how to swim even in water. He didn't see any sense whatever in trying to swim in ale, but before he could say so, Rose looked up from her plate frowning a little. "The nursery wants a good cleaning before then."

"The nursery is clean this minute, Rose," Nancy said. "Only this morning, I swept the hearth myself. Spick-and-span, it is. The king himself couldn't ask for a cleaner nursery."

"The quiet of the countryside, that's what her ladyship needs," Mr. Kimball said. "Good food, plenty of rest, and no fretting. We must all work hard to see Lady Schofield is well taken care of. A healthy child, safely delivered, means everything to the future of this family—and therefore to our own future here in the household."

"*When* in November do they expect the baby?" asked Rose. "The fifth of November would be good. Bonfire Night."

Nancy giggled. "Before the carriage was put away, the stable boys were making bets on the birth date. Go to them if you want a wager. You can pick the date or just bet if it will be a boy or a girl."

"Much good a girl would do us," said Rose. "Only a boy can inherit the title."

"Stop it!" said Bess. "It's only August. Months and months to go. Anything might go wrong in the meantime. Anything!"

"Quite right," said Mrs. Dutton. "Bad luck to behave as if this is all safely settled. Think of the trouble the poor lamb has had in the past."

"More than bad luck," said Mr. Kimball, "it is bad form. The peace and quiet of the countryside is all very well when doctors prescribe it to their patients. Don't make the mistake of thinking anyone has prescribed it for us. Our standards do not drop merely because we are away from London. Rose and Nancy, must I order you to leave the table? Stop that giggling."

"What trouble has Lady Schofield had?" Frederick leaned close enough to murmur to Bess. "What did you mean, anything might go wrong?"

Softly, Bess explained to Frederick. "This is the second time Lady Schofield has fallen pregnant. She lost the first baby. Last time, the moment the labor pains came on her ladyship, his lordship fell ill himself. Terrible, the misery he was in, and for once, no complaining from him, not a word."

"Not a word?" Frederick did not believe it. He knew Lord Schofield was free with complaints, often over the tiniest things. "Truly?"

"Yes, truly. Lord Schofield was as brave as could be, while her ladyship, well!" Bess was all admiration for Lady Schofield. "She was braver than that. She was like the Spartan lad who let a fox gnaw his vitals."

Frederick stared at Bess. "There was a fox?"

"No, of course there wasn't. Wait. I don't mean to confuse you. It's only a story," Bess explained. "Her maid told me. In ancient times, the Spartans trained their children never to admit to pain. A boy was caught with a fox—I can't remember what he was doing with a fox stuffed in his shirt, so don't ask me—and he never said a word, even though the fox chewed at him the whole time."

Mr. Kimball dismissed the servants, and everyone pushed back from the table still talking among themselves. The next chance he had, Frederick whispered to Bess, "Then what happened?"

Bess stopped clearing the table to gaze at Frederick. "It was dreadful. Sorrow and grief for months afterward. Lord and Lady Schofield were so sad."

"About the fox, I meant. What happened to the boy with the fox?"

"Oh, to the Spartan boy?" Bess went back to stacking dirty plates. "He died, of course."

"That's it? He died?" Frederick was disgusted. "That's a terrible story! And what's the point of it? Lady Schofield can't die. His lordship is a wizard. He wouldn't let her."

"Women do die in childbirth," Bess retorted. "It happens all the time."

"Not to rich women," Frederick insisted. "Not to ladies."

"Yes, it does so, and anything could happen to Lady Schofield," Bess whispered fiercely back. "If anything goes wrong, you can forget your promises. I won't tell your secret unless I must. But if Lady Schofield is in any danger, I shall. I'll tell everyone."

"Are you waiting for those plates to grow hands and wash themselves?" Mrs. Dutton demanded. "Away with you, Frederick, and let Bess get on with her work."

IN WHICH FREDERICK MEETS
HIS SECOND WIZARD

A week after Lord and Lady Schofield's arrival at Skeynes, a visitor arrived. Frederick was just tying Lord Schofield's cravat when Mr. Kimball, looking solemn as an owl, joined them.

"My lord, I regret to disturb you, but the mail coach has brought a—gentleman." Mr. Kimball hesitated over the word just long enough to make it plain that he didn't mean it. "He says his name is Pickering. He insists he is here because you summoned him. I've put him in the tapestry room."

"Pickering? Laurence Pickering? That's all? Those blockheads!" His cravat secured, Lord Schofield brushed Frederick aside to address Kimball. "I wrote to the Royal College of Wizards asking for them to send me the wizards who broke the spell on this place. But do they send me the eleven wizards? Do they send me ten? No! They send me one! Pickering!"

Eager to see even one of the wizards who had broken the Skeynes curse, Frederick followed Kimball as Kimball followed Lord Schofield downstairs to the tapestry room. There, folded up into a corner of one of the armchairs, they found a skinny young man, more than half asleep. When Hetty had talked about wizards, she had made this one, Mr. Pickering of the torn sleeve, with his fondness for her mother's pastry, seem almost like an ordinary person. Frederick could see why Mr. Kimball had been doubtful about the man's social position. The clothes he wore were too old to be fashionable, but although soiled by the journey, they were well cut and well cared for. Frederick suspected Mr. Pickering's chin had not yet seen a razor that day, but his fair hair was clean and combed.

"Pickering!" Lord Schofield loomed over his visitor. "It is the height of rudeness to fall asleep during a social call."

Frederick knew from the tone of Lord Schofield's voice that his employer was annoyed but not truly angry. From the way Mr. Pickering completely ignored his host, it looked as if the newcomer knew it too.

Eventually Pickering stirred and yawned. When at last he opened his eyes, it seemed that his first and only concern in the world was to polish and adjust his spectacles.

Frederick felt deep admiration for Mr. Pickering's

air of calmness. If he had been a complete stranger to the scene and asked to guess which of the two men was a lord, Frederick would have put his money on Mr. Pickering.

When Mr. Pickering was finally satisfied with the condition of his eyeglasses, he gazed mildly up at Lord Schofield. "But I haven't come here on a social call. Far from it. You sent for me. You said it was a matter of the gravest urgency."

"I? Sent for you?" Lord Schofield took the armchair opposite. "I did no such thing."

For a moment, Lord Schofield's denial took Frederick's breath away. Then he perceived that the two men were joking with each other.

"You did. You wrote to the Royal College of Wizards demanding a further consultation on a matter of domestic spell-breaking." Pickering sighed a little. "That is why I spent much of last night and all of this morning atop a coach, rattling my bones along the Bath road for your benefit. Have I suffered merely to gratify a whim you've since forgotten you had?"

"I see you haven't changed in the slightest. Still completely useless until you've been fed." Lord Schofield turned to Mr. Kimball and Frederick. "Kimball, see to our guest. He's hardly what I'd hoped for, but we must make the best of what little the Royal College of Wizards has seen fit to send us."

"Very good, my lord." Mr. Kimball bowed to Lord Schofield and Mr. Pickering before he turned to Frederick. "Show Mr. Pickering to the blue room, Frederick, then fetch him towels and hot water so he can make himself more comfortable. I will have a breakfast tray prepared and sent up at once."

Frederick marveled at the way Mr. Kimball's whole attitude toward the young man had changed. Now anyone would think young Mr. Pickering was royalty. So this was what a real wizard was like.

Frederick led Mr. Pickering upstairs to the blue room, the most comfortable of the guest bedchambers, and brought him soap and a razor along with the towels and hot water.

Mr. Pickering thanked Frederick and set about cleaning up. Frederick hovered at the door, reluctant to cut short the chance to talk to a real wizard.

"If you're waiting for me to tip you, I'm sorry. I haven't a farthing to spare," said Mr. Pickering.

"No, sir!" Frederick gathered his wits. "I was just wondering if there was anything else you need."

"Of course you were," Mr. Pickering agreed. "Very dutiful of you. Frederick, that's what you're called, isn't it? I've been promised breakfast as soon as possible, so there's nothing else I need just now. But even if there were, I still don't have the means to tip you." He devoted his full attention to drying his face.

Frederick stayed put.

Mr. Pickering looked up from the towel. "Was there something else?"

"Are you truly one of the wizards who broke the curse on this place?"

"I am." Mr. Pickering didn't seem to find anything unusual in Frederick's question. "It was my first official assignment. I'm not likely to forget it. Strictly speaking, it was a curse on Lord Schofield, not on the house itself. If you and your colleagues are concerned for your safety, you needn't be."

"Not my safety," Frederick said. "Lady Schofield's."

"Ah." Mr. Pickering looked thoughtful. "I cannot tell you anything about the spell until I've had a chance to discuss it with his lordship, but let me reassure you. If there were any danger to Lady Schofield whatsoever, there would be at least ten other wizards here with me, possibly more."

"So the curse isn't a danger?" Frederick asked.

"I'm not at liberty to discuss the curse with anyone until I've discussed it with Lord Schofield. Perhaps not even then." Mr. Pickering smiled at Frederick. The suddenness of it transformed his face, made him look hardly more than a boy himself. "But don't you worry. Skeynes has magic of its own. For every curse ever laid on this place, there have been at least seven spells of blessing cast to counter it."

Frederick was on pins and needles lest Mr. Pickering help Lord Schofield detect Billy Bly's presence at Skeynes. But late that afternoon, when Lord Schofield had finally finished his private consultation with Mr. Pickering, all he said when he summoned Frederick to his workroom was, "You may tidy up for us, Frederick. Take extra care when you clean the floor. Don't miss anything."

Despite a large breakfast and a thorough scrub, Mr. Pickering was looking sleepier than ever. He had arranged himself in the corner nearest the fireplace and was paging slowly through a stack of books he'd selected from Lord Schofield's shelves. "There's nothing to worry about," he said without taking his attention from the book before him. "As ever, the Royal College of Wizards stands by its work."

Frederick admired Mr. Pickering's confidence. Lord Schofield seemed less impressed. "As ever, the Royal College of Wizards stands by its own good opinion of itself. But in this instance, I think I can trust it. That is, I trust *you*."

"You'd better. At least you can be certain I was properly trained, having done most of the groundwork yourself." Mr. Pickering opened another book and held it side by side with the first, comparing them critically, before closing the first book and devoting himself to the second. "I owe you a great deal."

Frederick had never imagined that Lord Schofield had trained Mr. Pickering. Intent on learning as much as possible, he worked as slowly as he dared.

"Poppycock. I taught you alpha and beta, and very little more. As soon as possible, I turned you over to Mitchell. He did the heavy lifting." Lord Schofield considered for a moment. "Or rather, you did. Mitchell is renowned for his wizardry, but as an instructor, he's a steep climb uphill."

Frederick swept the same bit of floor over and over again. If he moved, Lord Schofield might remember he was there and stop gossiping.

"Mr. Mitchell can be an excellent instructor," said Mr. Pickering. "But if not for you, I would have had no instructor whatever. I would be polishing some other officer's boots for him at this very moment."

"Nonsense. You couldn't possibly be in the army. Your eyesight isn't good enough." Despite his scornful tone, Lord Schofield looked pleased. "Frederick, if you sweep that spot much longer, you'll wear a hole through the floor. Get on with it!"

Mr. Pickering said, "I still consider you my first tutor. At the Royal College of Wizards, you have gained a reputation as a man with a keen eye for magical talent. I did my best not to let you down."

Lord Schofield beamed. "Too clever by half, Pickering."

Mr. Pickering smiled gently back. "Thank you, my lord."

"What! Is that a bit of common courtesy I hear from you at last? Be careful, or I shall think your egalitarian principles are slipping."

"Old habits die hard." As Frederick swept near his feet, Mr. Pickering closed the book he was reading and returned to his original subject. "Since there's no danger to you or Lady Schofield, there's no cause for concern."

"What on earth are you talking about?" Lord Schofield demanded. At a meaningful look from Mr. Pickering he hesitated. Then, prompted by an equally meaningful nod from Mr. Pickering, Lord Schofield continued in his most patient tone, as if he were addressing a clergyman. "Ah. Just so. No cause for concern. The spell was broken properly and disposed of professionally."

For a moment, Frederick wondered if they had lost their wits. Then he decided they were speaking for his benefit. They expected him to gossip. This way he could reassure the other servants in the household.

"Only a stubborn residue remains." Mr. Pickering smiled at Frederick as he shifted his feet to avoid the broom. "Not much danger there."

"*No* danger there," said Lord Schofield. "I would need to forget every protective spell I ever knew before what residue remains presented any threat to me. More than that, every protective counter-charm on this place would have to fail at once. I have no intention of leaving this house until Kate's child is safely here. Furthermore, the counter-charms blessing this house will outlast the stones it is made of by several centuries. If any of the servants ask you, Frederick, you may quote me."

In other words, there was no need for anyone to fear the curse. No need for any further gossip about it, either. Frederick knew exactly what he had just been told, but he kept his expression blank as he looked up from his work. "Me, my lord? Who would ever ask me anything?"

"Who indeed, Frederick?" Lord Schofield raised an eyebrow. Once again, Frederick had the sense his employer was looking clear through him, seeing more than Frederick wanted anyone to see.

"We have had an afternoon of it, haven't we?" Mr. Pickering sighed gently. "I don't suppose there's any chance of a cup of tea and a morsel of pastry, is there?"

"Food again." Lord Schofield looked resigned. "Put those books away, Pickering, and I'll ring for Kimball. We must make sure you don't wither away from hunger. At least, not before dinner is served."

IN WHICH FREDERICK
ISSUES A CALL

Two weeks passed, with daily private consultations held—and cleaned up afterward by Frederick—and no mention of Billy Bly whatever. Lord Schofield pronounced himself satisfied. Frederick was sorry to see Mr. Pickering go, and not only because he left no tip.

Mr. Pickering had shown Frederick it was possible to be a wizard without being a nobleman. It was possible, although obviously challenging, to be a wizard without being a rich man. It was even possible to be a wizard without being old, for Mr. Pickering had been a wizard at least since the night Sir Hilary's curse upon Lord Schofield was broken, yet even now he was barely four and twenty years of age.

Frederick had learned the young man's age when he was sent back to Hetty the seamstress. Mr. Kimball had ordered him a new suit of livery, but the London outfitters had sent coat and breeches too big for him in every way. Hetty was to make it fit until Frederick grew into it.

"Hard to credit, isn't it? A lad so young already a full-fledged wizard." Hetty double-checked Frederick's measurements and began to pin the fabric. "He must have worked ever so hard."

"He read the whole time he was here," said Frederick. "One night, when Bess brought him his dinner on a tray, she watched through the keyhole while he was eating. He never took his nose out of the book the whole time."

Hetty didn't seem a bit surprised. "Ever so learned, wizards need to be. I expect he works hard just to keep up."

"Lord Schofield was Mr. Pickering's very first magic teacher." Frederick hoped that a bit of fresh information would earn some matching gossip from Hetty, but she kept right on pinning his clothes. "He says there's nothing left of the curse but residue. Just scraps of the curse. Lord Schofield can manage residue with ease."

"To gossip about such matters is to give them strength. You know I won't speak of such things, so don't tease me." Hetty kept working. "It only stands to reason. The more you pick at a blister, the longer it takes to heal."

After a long silence, Frederick gave up and played

his trump card. "Mr. Pickering was Lord Schofield's servant back when his lordship was in the army."

"Was he?" Hetty didn't sound very surprised. "He must have been only a few years older than you are now, then. Fancy that. No wonder he had such a taste for my mother's pastry. He was still just a growing lad." Hetty stepped back to survey her work. "There now. Look at how you've grown! I'll have my work cut out for me with the coat, but your legs are so long, your new breeches nearly fit just as they are."

Frederick's fidgeting efforts to see what she meant only made the pins scratch him. "They don't feel as if they fit."

"Give it a chance." Hetty helped him out of the coat. "Put the old ones on and be off with you. I need to work."

◦◯◦

Mr. Pickering's visit had made Lord Schofield less willing than usual to venture away from Skeynes. Even after the young wizard's departure, he still spent most days closeted in his workroom. This meant that by day Frederick had fewer duties as assistant valet.

"You haven't pestered me to learn anything new in weeks," Piers announced one morning in late September. "But I've thought of something I can teach you."

Lord Schofield, his cravat freshly tied, had just gone

off about his day's business. The dressing room was still littered with items left from the shave Piers had given his employer. Frederick had five discarded neck cloths to be laundered, pressed, and put away, and his lordship's second-best boots to polish. "Yes, sir. Right away, sir."

"You don't look too pleased." Piers made himself comfortable in Lord Schofield's chair. "I'm not to teach you how to give a proper shave until you have begun to grow whiskers yourself. Kimball's orders. But I can teach you how to sharpen a razor. That will save a good deal of time every day."

"That will save *you* a good deal of time every day," said Frederick.

"Less of your sauce." Piers opened the case containing Lord Schofield's matched straight razors. "Behold. Before you lies death and disfigurement."

Frederick studied the steel and ivory implements gleaming against the black plush lining of the case. "That's odd. Looks like a bunch of razors to me."

"No clowning, you. A razor means danger. In the wrong hands, that is." Piers selected one of the razors, opened it, and held it up so the wickedly sharp blade caught the light. "In the hands of an expert barber, a razor of good Sheffield steel provides a close shave for his client and an honest means of earning a living for the barber."

Piers tilted the razor this way and that as they admired the play of light on steel in silence. Then Piers shook himself a little and returned to his lecture topic. "Mind how you handle these. Use one carelessly and you will deserve the beating I'll give you for it."

"Yes, sir." Frederick knew Piers was not joking.

"There's an art to honing a razor. For now, you'll leave that to me. What I need you to do is clean the razor I use on his lordship each morning. Today, that will be this one." Piers handed the razor to Frederick with care. "I've already cleaned it. You can strop it now, get the edge back."

Frederick didn't tell Piers he already knew how to sharpen knives. Razors could not be very different, but there would be no convincing Piers of that. "Why are there seven razors? Lord Schofield only has one chin."

"Ah, but he's young yet." Piers showed Frederick how to use the strop. "Hook it there, that's right. Now hold the other end in your left hand. Make sure the edge of the razor is away from you. Draw it along the leather. Not quite so sharp an angle. You'll nick the strop. That's better."

Frederick worked hard to memorize every detail of what Piers was showing him. When he had the attention to spare, he asked again, "Why so many razors?"

"The blade needs a rest between shaves. So there's a razor for each day of the week." Piers adjusted Frederick's grip on the razor. "That's right. Never let the edge come toward you. Careful."

Frederick found the knack of it. Soon he was stropping and flipping the razor with hardly a break in rhythm.

"That's good." Piers took the razor back and held it so they could both inspect the edge. "You want to keep the edge as sharp and fine as possible. Turn the edge ever so slightly, and the sharpness is gone. You'll have to hone the razor all over again. Treat it right, a razor only needs its edge honed four times a year. Treat it wrong, and you've made it into a very expensive bit of scrap metal. The cost will be stopped from your wages."

"That's it for stropping, then?" Frederick asked. "What about cleaning? Do I wash it with soap and water?"

"Rinse it," Piers answered. "Rinse it clean and blot it dry. Like this. Don't scrub at it with the towel. It's a fine piece of steel, not your silly face. Always remember—the important thing is the edge. When the steel is dry, rub it with mineral oil, same as you would a good cooking pot. Don't use too much oil and don't rub it too much. Remember—"

"The edge, the edge." Frederick nodded. "I remember."

"The other thing to watch for is rust. If you ever

notice even a speck of rust on the blade, here's what you do." Piers went through every detail of the care required to keep a razor in good condition. Frederick paid close attention, even though it did not seem complicated or difficult. It was painstaking, but he had always been particularly good at taking pains.

᧬

Razor lessons took a long time. As a result, Frederick was late finishing up the neck cloths. As he hung the spotless strips of linen to dry, Frederick wished that Billy Bly was there to help him. He had done all he could to conceal the brownie's presence at Skeynes. Now it seemed wasted effort. There was little to tell that Billy Bly had ever been there at all. Not since Lord and Lady Schofield's arrival had Frederick heard the rustle like wind in the trees, the sound he associated with Billy Bly's presence. Not since then had he felt the sense of companionship when Billy Bly was near. For all he had seen of Billy Bly of late, Frederick thought, he might as well have let Lord Schofield banish him again.

Sometimes, when he was certain Lord Schofield was not in the house, Frederick called Billy Bly. He dared not raise his voice above a whisper, but he called the brownie's name, longing for his companionship. No answer ever came. Brownies, it seemed, did not come when they were called.

Frederick had been alone as long as he could remember. Since he had never known anything different, it had not troubled him. Now, living in a house packed with busy people, he felt lonely. Sometimes he missed Billy Bly's companionship so much, he wished he had never had it in the first place.

Frederick complained to Bess one day as she helped him air out Lord Schofield's bedchamber. "I wonder sometimes if Billy Bly was anything but a dream."

Hands on hips, Bess regarded him with deep displeasure. "If he was only a dream, I shall give you such a wigging."

Frederick handed her a stack of freshly aired bed linen. "There's been no sign of him since he gave me the warning about the curse. Nothing."

Bess set about making up the side of the bed nearest her. "Perhaps that nice Mr. Pickering banished him while he was consulting on the curse."

"Without a word?" Frederick made up his side of the bed. Working with Bess made it an easy task. They smoothed linens and tucked blankets in as if they had been practicing together for years. "Wouldn't he have mentioned it, at least?"

"Perhaps he did. Perhaps he told Lord Schofield in private." Bess put the finishing touches to the bed and moved on to the cushions on the furniture. She gave each plump feather pillow a few slaps, as if she were spanking it, then placed it to look its best.

Frederick picked a last bit of lint off the freshly swept carpet. "If Lord Schofield knew Billy Bly was here, wouldn't he have shouted at me about it? Done something?"

"Why should he?" Bess had her hands on her hips again, but this time she was surveying the bedchamber with approval. "It's his house, after all. He does as he pleases. If I had to guess, I'd say Billy Bly is playing least in sight because he's ashamed of how he lied to you over the curse. And so he should be, too."

"Perhaps he is. Oh, I wish I could see Billy Bly again. I wouldn't even ask him any questions. I just want to know he's all right." Frederick sighed. "Thanks for the help."

"Don't mention it," said Bess. "You promised you'd help me with the cobwebs in the big pantry."

"So I did," Frederick said. Even to his own ears, he sounded a bit hollow.

"Now would be an excellent time to dust for cobwebs," Bess hinted broadly.

Frederick didn't have the heart to argue.

Another month passed and Frederick detected no sign of Billy Bly. Summer gave up and autumn took its place. Not so much as a speck of soot appeared where it was not supposed to be. Frederick heard no squeaks whatsoever. The only roaring came from Lord Schofield. Those occasions were all related to the tightness of his cravat or the closeness of his shave.

In his heart, Frederick knew perfectly well that Billy Bly was no dream. He went over every detail he remembered about Billy Bly, from his fondness for fresh cream to his love of counting.

I could no more walk away from counting mustard seeds than I could walk into a church on Easter morning. That's what Billy Bly had said, the night Lord Schofield conjured him into a chalk circle and banished him from the London house.

Frederick went to the kitchens to talk to Grant. He chose his moment with care, at a time when Grant was not so busy that he would shout at Frederick to go away, but not so much at leisure that he would want to know any details about the need for mustard plasters. He chose the time well, for Grant let him have half a cup of mustard seeds with not a single question asked.

The next time he was left alone to sleep in Lord Schofield's dressing room, Frederick pulled out the mustard seeds. He'd tied them in an old silk stocking, clean but worn, one of Lord Schofield's discards.

It was late on a rainy night, when all Lord Schofield's clothes were put away, when the floor was swept, and the fire in the hearth burned down to embers, with all the household gone to sleep, Frederick untied the knot.

"Billy Bly, Billy Bly," said Frederick softly as he held the stocking by the toe and shook out the seeds on the floor, "please come to me."

The mustard seeds were small and dark. They bounced and scattered much farther into the corners of the dressing room than he'd expected. They had a sharp scent to them. Frederick knew he had his work cut out for him, trying to clean spilled mustard seed so thoroughly that Lord Schofield would never guess what he'd done.

"Billy Bly," Frederick whispered, "please come."

For a moment, all was still. The only sound was the sound of rain and the hush of the wind outside.

"Frederick!" The door opened with such force, it banged against the wall. Lord Schofield walked in, candle held high, and his scowl was terrible. "What do you think you are doing?"

Frederick stared up at him, mute with fear. The darkness of the room balanced the glow of embers on the hearth, the brightness of that single candle. The sharp scent of mustard seed crushed by Lord Schofield's tread mixed with the sudden sweat of fear that pricked him all over.

Lord Schofield was waiting for an answer, and the only sound in the room was the spatter of rain on the windows.

Frederick's fear was eased by a twist of pure anger. Who did this man think he was, bellowing down at a boy half his size? For a moment, his rage distracted him from his terror. It calmed him enough he could choke out an answer. "I was trying to call Billy Bly, my lord."

"In my dressing room?" Lord Schofield roared. "Without permission?"

"Yes, my lord." Frederick met Lord Schofield's wrath with defiance. "I wasn't calling him here from London. He is already at Skeynes, my lord."

"Is he? Yet you never thought to mention it." Lord Schofield's voice had gentled, but his anger was plain.

"I knew you'd only banish him again. But he followed me here. He followed me." Frederick had to break off to steady his voice. He was not about to cry. Not if it killed him. When he had conquered the lump in his throat, he continued. "Billy Bly it was who warned me about the curse. That's why I couldn't tell you how I knew. But ever since Mr. Pickering came and said it was all just residue, Billy Bly is nowhere to be found."

"So you set out to call him." Lord Schofield studied the seeds scattered across the floor. "That has the ring of truth, at least."

Frederick's anger rose again. "I don't tell lies, sir. I wanted to see Billy Bly again, just to make sure he was all right. And perhaps to ask him about the residue, to make sure that was all right too." Frederick blew his nose on the silk stocking, crumpled it up, and put it in his pocket. "I'm sacked, aren't I?"

"I think that's the least you deserve, don't you?" Lord Schofield. "Sweep up that mustard seed and come with me to the workroom. We have much to discuss."

IN WHICH FREDERICK LEARNS
THE FIRST THING ABOUT MAGIC

In his days at the orphanage, Frederick had sometimes been awake far into the night. Back then, he knew he had nothing to fear. Darkness was just darkness. But that October night the wizard's workroom looked much darker and larger than usual, the ceiling much higher. As he followed Lord Schofield downstairs to his workroom, the shadows cast by the flickering candle grew deeper by the moment. The rattling at the windows seemed more than just the wind outside.

"Lock the door." While Frederick put his dustpan of mustard seeds carefully on the worktable, Lord Schofield lit lamps around the room. "I suppose it's my own fault, for not guessing you had such a fascination with magic. If you dared to set out to summon Billy Bly with no more than a handful of mustard seeds and no training whatsoever, I think you are in dire need of a lesson in the *dangers* of magic. Just this once, I'll show you."

Caught between joy at the attention and fear for his job, Frederick helped Lord Schofield assemble the materials for the spell. The wizard lectured Frederick all the while he gathered his tools.

"First you must clean your work space, and not just the spot you'll use for the spell. Clean the entire surface. Floors are best. You can't fall off the floor. While you clean, you must think clearly about what you're about to do."

Frederick nodded. He was afraid to speak, lest Lord Schofield stop talking and start to roar again.

"Once you have a clean work surface, you must define the boundary of the spell's influence. Chalk is good, but use what you like. If you have any choice, choose to keep it small. Ground the spell. Use four elements and six directions."

"Six?" Frederick asked.

"East, west, north, south, up, and down."

"Oh." Chastened, Frederick hesitated but could not help asking another question. "Will I need to use a wand?"

Lord Schofield didn't look up from his work. "If a spell should demand it, a wand could be used. One may use almost anything. I once witnessed a spell that stopped an armed man in his tracks and held him fast for ten minutes, a spell that was cast with nothing but a daisy-chain. Don't try it. Such elegance requires great skill and great strength of will. Someone like you should keep things as simple as possible. No wand."

Frederick asked, "I'd just wave my hands, then?"

"Not even that until you are grounded. Remember, all this time you are fixing your position, you *must* keep the purpose and meaning of your spell firmly in mind. When you are grounded and have the whole structure of the thing clear, then you may cast the spell. Not until then, or you will find yourself dealing with inequalities inside and outside the area you've chosen." As Lord Schofield nattered on, the shadows of the workroom grew less threatening. It became just another room, and watching the magic was like watching anything else.

Frederick soon discovered the first thing he needed to know about magic was that Lord Schofield had to be stopped from distracting them both with explanations of more advanced things to know about how to cast a spell. The best way to keep Lord Schofield on the subject was to ask him questions. "How?"

At Lord Schofield's glare, Frederick rephrased his question. "I mean, how do I cast the spell? What do I say exactly?"

Lord Schofield's glare mellowed into an everyday withering look. "If you think I'm going to give you some sort of motto or a special enchanted word to blurt out whenever the fancy strikes you, you may think again."

"But what do I say?" Frederick persisted.

"What you would say would be dictated by what you intended. For our purpose tonight, we will confine ourselves to the simplest measures. Just the imperative verb—for you command, do you see?—and the name of whoever it is you dare to command."

"Impera—" Frederick broke off. "What?"

"Imperative. Never mind. Keep it simple. *Come.* How is that?"

"So I say 'come' and 'Billy Bly'? That's it?"

"That's it."

"And that's casting the spell?"

"In part. The moment you call the name, cast the mustard seeds into the area you have delineated—"

"Delin—" Frederick gave up and just pointed to the floor between them. "You mean the circle you drew with chalk?"

Lord Schofield sighed. "Yes."

"And that's casting the spell?"

"Not entirely. Meanwhile, you must balance the flux of force within the area you have delineated—" At Frederick's unspoken confusion, Lord Schofield broke off and tried again. "Inside the circle, I mean. Balance that against the flux of force outside the circle. Unless you truly study the theory, you must at all costs remain outside the circle yourself. Including yourself in the interior flux of force complicates matters."

Frederick held up his hand. "How?"

Lord Schofield hunted for words simple enough to explain. Finally, he said, "It makes it more dangerous."

"Oh."

"Precisely. Oh. Stay outside the O."

With care, Frederick and Lord Schofield worked together through the steps. Frederick understood Lord Schofield's instructions better once he saw the actions he took, but he did not understand any of the words Lord Schofield muttered. "What's that you're saying?"

"An incantation. An incantation is a set of sounds intended to help me focus."

"Oh. Magic words, you mean. Aren't you going to teach me?"

Lord Schofield growled. "No, I am not going to teach you a magical incantation. If you think I'm being unfair, too bad."

At last, with the chalk circle drawn, with Frederick's thoughts as focused as he could make them, with Lord Schofield's mumbling a constant undertone, Frederick called, "Come, Billy Bly," and scattered the mustard seeds in the circle.

Nothing happened. Frederick felt silly. Lord Schofield kept on with the muttered incantation. Then Frederick saw the air over the circle shimmer, but it might have been the candle flames fluttering. Frederick closed his eyes hard and opened them wide for another look. The shimmer was still there.

Then the light of every lamp and candle in the room jumped and guttered at once. The shadows remade themselves, and the mustard seeds scattered as if blown by a bellows. Seeds skittered across the floor in every direction to disappear into the shifting gloom.

Frederick was filled with wonder. The spell may not have worked, but it did something. His very first try! In a quiet corner of his brain, Frederick found time to admire the steadiness of Lord Schofield's mumble. The wizard didn't falter. The air shimmered again, and there was Billy Bly in the circle, wearing something like a shiny black belt around his middle.

But that was wrong, Frederick knew. Something about that belt was wrong. No. Everything about that black thing was very wrong.

Twisting and turning, yellowed teeth bared, Billy Bly struggled with the belt and drew one end of it up to his mouth. His teeth were nothing like human, shiny and small but wickedly sharp. He bit at the belt. Once his teeth were clamped in it, he shook his head, worrying at the black thing. Like a dog with a rabbit, he shook the belt.

Not a belt, Frederick understood. Not a snake either, although it resembled a snake as it twisted this way and that.

The black thing coiled tighter. With a low whine of pain, Billy Bly doubled up and fell to his knees.

Lord Schofield called out a word Frederick didn't understand. The mere sound of it made every lamp and candle burn more brightly for a moment.

With a sound like a whip-crack and a smell like wet ashes, the black thing was gone. Billy Bly was alone, sitting in the center of the chalk circle, spitting and gasping for breath.

"Billy Bly!" Frederick felt his heart lurch with joy and concern at the brownie's reappearance. "Are you hurt?"

When the brownie had recovered enough to answer, his deep voice rumbled indignantly. "It got away. You let it get away! I had it! It was at my—my mercy!"

"Was it indeed? I beg your pardon. Appearances can be so misleading," said Lord Schofield. "Thank you for coming at our call."

"*It* nearly had *you*!" Careful to stay outside the chalk circle, Frederick crouched down as close to Billy Bly as he dared. "Are you all right?"

Still catching his breath, Billy Bly nodded. Cheerful as a fox, he grinned at Frederick as he panted. "You again."

"Was that it?" Frederick asked. He kept his voice soft, as if mentioning it would call it back again. "Was that thing the curse?"

"Residue of the curse," Lord Schofield corrected. At Frederick's look of disbelief, he raised his eyebrows. "Mere residue."

"It tasted bad. Bitter." Recovered, Billy Bly stood. "Right, then. I'll be off."

"You won't." Lord Schofield loomed over them. "Talk. Tell me why you are here."

Frederick looked up at his employer and held his ground in silence, sheltering the brownie with his body. He wouldn't let anyone threaten Billy Bly, not even Lord Schofield.

"I take orders from no mortal." Billy Bly shut his mouth with a snap and glared up at the wizard.

"We don't want to give you orders. We just want to know what to do," Frederick assured Billy Bly. "Please help us."

Billy Bly said nothing. Every line of his body made his defiance clear.

"He's hungry. Just like Pickering. Useless until you feed him. Nip down to the kitchen and find him something to eat. I'll hold the spell steady for you." Lord Schofield handed Frederick an oil lantern. "Bring some brandy with you."

Small chance of finding food and drink at that

hour, Frederick knew. He didn't waste breath questioning his orders. Fortunately, when he closed down the kitchens for the night, it was Mr. Grant's custom to leave out a dish of cream. Frederick knew where to look for the saucer. He brought back the cream, half a loaf of bread, three apples, and the brandy decanter from Lord Schofield's bedchamber—all the rest of the brandy in the house was kept locked up. Mr. Kimball had the key, but Frederick didn't fancy waking him to explain why he needed it.

"I won't eat your food," Billy Bly told Lord Schofield when Frederick returned, arms full.

"I thought you might feel that way," Lord Schofield replied. "Very well. I give this food to Frederick. Will you accept it from him?"

"I give it gladly," Frederick added.

Billy Bly thought it over a moment longer, then yielded. "I could do with a morsel, I'll grant you that."

When the food and drink had been distributed, the brandy to Lord Schofield and everything else set before Billy Bly, Frederick settled back into his place beside the chalk circle.

"Ready?" Lord Schofield asked him. "Balance the circle, then."

Frederick did his best to do as he was told. When Lord Schofield was satisfied, the spell eased in around him. Little by little, the air in the room seemed to thicken. To Frederick, the place grew heavy with smells. He almost tasted each bite of bread and apple, every sip of cream that Billy Bly lapped from the saucer. When Lord Schofield poured more brandy, the sharp scent made Frederick's eyes water.

Billy Bly licked his fingers clean of cream and any crumb of bread, then pocketed the last apple as he pushed the empty saucer away.

"Better?" asked Lord Schofield. "Now, where were we? Oh, yes. You were to speak."

When Lord Schofield said the word *speak,* Frederick felt it as a shiver deep in his bones even as he heard it with his ears. Billy Bly crouched low, flinching from it.

"Stop it," said Billy Bly. "I came here uninvited, but I don't deserve punishment. On your behalf, I have hunted this creature. Day and night I keep it in check lest it trouble those in your care."

"You came here to hunt?" Lord Schofield asked.

"No. I followed Frederick," Billy Bly replied. "I like him."

Touched by this, Frederick tried to reassure him. "There's no need to worry. Lord Schofield knows enough magic to protect himself, and the creature poses no danger to anyone else."

Billy Bly glared at Lord Schofield and made a rude noise. "I did not come to the countryside in search of sport. But when rats are in the grain, one must hunt."

"You hunt nothing but the dregs of a broken spell," said Lord Schofield. "Let it go. When you make it your prey, you lend it strength."

"Let it go? How can I?" Billy Bly indicated the mustard seeds scattered in the corners of the work-room. "As well ask me not to count these seeds. What I begin, I must finish. This creature, whatever you choose to call it, has free run of your dwelling. That cannot be."

"Enough." Lord Schofield took off his coat and rolled up his sleeves. "I will not rest until I have freed you from this quest of yours. I'll cleanse us of this resi-due tonight."

"Before you call it back, free me." Billy Bly made the spell holding him shake. Frederick felt it as a prickle moving through him just beneath the skin. "Release me. Please."

With a wave of his hand, Lord Schofield let the sum-moning spell go. Thrown off balance as it melted away, Frederick rocked back on his heels and then sat down hard on the floor. There was a sharp scent of mustard and he knew he had crushed some of the seeds as he landed. His keener senses were gone, vanished with the spell that had brought them.

"I thank you, sir." Billy Bly remained crouching in the chalk circle, watching Lord Schofield mistrustfully.

"You are, within limits, welcome." Lord Schofield rubbed his hands. "Now. Let's rid ourselves of this nonsense once and for all."

Frederick helped by fetching equipment as Lord Schofield prepared to cast a second spell. He could see similarities to the first. Lord Schofield drew a much larger chalk ring on the floor. Because he was watching for it, Frederick saw Lord Schofield's quick gestures up and down and to each point of the compass. The rest of the spell was done too quickly for Frederick to follow. Lord Schofield muttered his incantation. Frederick strained his ears but could not make sense of a single word of it.

Stillness filled the room. Heat gathered as Lord Schofield muttered. The smell of mustard faded. The stink of mold replaced it. The room grew cold. Then every candle flame shuddered and nearly went out. From the corner of his eye, Frederick thought he saw the shadows move. One moment the chalk circle was empty and the next it held a coiled serpent, the sleek black thing Billy Bly had struggled with before.

Frederick felt the back of his neck turn cold. Billy Bly stayed in his place but he bristled at the sight of the thing.

Lord Schofield roared another word Frederick did not understand. The black thing dwindled into itself. It shrank. The chill and stink in the air faded as the black thing grew smaller and smaller. Warmer and warmer the room became, and the scent of mold gave way once more to the friendlier smell of mustard. The candle flames grew tall again. Frederick felt the back of his neck return to normal.

When there was nothing left in the ring but a handful of ashes, Lord Schofield said no word that Frederick heard, made no sound, nor moved so much as a fingertip. Yet the spell shifted. For an instant, Frederick felt the magic shift as surely if he himself were holding the spell. The ashes vanished. Nothing remained in the spell's chalk circle, not so much as a fleck of soot.

Frederick frowned. Hadn't Billy Bly said bits of it came off easily? Strange that Lord Schofield's spell hadn't made more of a mess.

Lord Schofield sighed and straightened. He looked old and tired as he called for soap and a basin of water and washed his hands. As he took the towel from Frederick, he murmured, "I haven't felt such hate in years. I hope I never encounter it again."

To Billy Bly, Lord Schofield said, "I thank you for your kind vigilance."

Billy Bly bowed to him. "Thank you for cleansing this place. May we all, at last, find rest." With that, he was gone, leaving behind only the sound of leaves rustling louder than the patter of rain on the windows.

Before the rustling sound had quite faded, a soft tap came at the door. Scowling at the interruption, Lord Schofield answered it to find Lady Schofield there. "My dear Kate, what are you doing here at this hour? Why aren't you in bed?"

Lady Schofield, wrapped in a lacy woolen shawl over a thick dressing gown, looked even more enormous than usual. Her wedding ring gleamed in the lamplight as she held up her left hand to halt his words. "My dear Thomas, I came to see what on earth you have been doing to give yourself such a headache. I was in bed. It's your own fault I've come to pester you." Behind Lady Schofield, her maid Reardon stood by with another shawl. Behind Reardon, Frederick just glimpsed Bess.

"As you can plainly see, there is no need to fuss." Lord Schofield did not permit Lady Schofield or the maids to cross the threshold. "Now, back to bed with you."

"It's as I said, my lady," Reardon murmured. "A tempest in a teapot. As usual."

"Oh, Thomas." Lady Schofield brushed past her husband to enter the workroom. She stood close to Frederick as she inspected the chalk marks on the floor, close enough Frederick caught the scent of cedar and lavender from the wraps bundled around her. "I never truly worry until you tell me there is no need to fuss.

You've done a spell, haven't you? A substantial one? You look quite done up."

"No such thing," said Lord Schofield. "I never get headaches."

Bess was watching Frederick instead of Lord and Lady Schofield. She waggled her eyebrows at him in inquiry. Frederick was glad the snake thing had been banished and that Billy Bly had taken his leave before they were disturbed. Much easier to explain everything that way. He made a "tell you later" face at Bess. She gave him a "mind you do or there will be trouble" look back.

"No, of course you don't. Silly of me." Lady Schofield turned from her inspection of the workroom to stand before her husband. "I love this house. It would take a great deal to frighten me away." Lady Schofield looked down at herself. "I'm not easy to move just now. But you would tell me if there were some reason I should leave, wouldn't you? I could stay in the village. Some of the neighbors have invited me to stay with them, should I wish it. That's how far the rumors have run, Thomas. Even the neighbors worry about us living here with the curse."

Lord Schofield put his hands on his wife's shoulders. "Sir Hilary Bedrick is dead. His spell can't hurt anyone anymore. I've banished the last of it, Kate. Put up with the neighbors if you wish. I'll take you anywhere you please. But there's no need. Skeynes is safe. I've made it safe."

"Yes." Lady Schofield put her hands over his. "At what cost I can guess. Very well. I'll go back to bed, Thomas. Work as late as you must. But when you've finished, come tell me good night."

"Good morning, more likely," said Lord Schofield wryly. "Perhaps it wasn't a large spell, but it went very deep."

Lady Schofield took her leave, Reardon and Bess in her wake. Lord Schofield locked the door and leaned against it. "Women. Sometimes they scare me to death."

"What now?" Frederick asked.

"What do you think? Casting the spell is but half the work done." Lord Schofield took up a broom. "Now comes the other half, cleaning up every trace of the magic."

Frederick sighed and reached for his dustpan. "Housework, that's what magic amounts to. Lucky I'm good at it."

IN WHICH FREDERICK IS
ORDERED TO HUNT RATS

That night, Frederick could not sleep. Lord Schofield's words rattled around in his head like peas and beans. Over and over he thumped his straw mattress into a different shape, each shape lumpier than the last, until Frederick heard a rooster crowing. He buried his face in his hands. The sun would be up before he was asleep. "I give up."

"You don't," said Billy Bly from the far corner of the dressing room. "That's one reason I liked you from the first."

"You!" Frederick lit a candle. "Where have you been?"

"Harvest season, isn't it?" Billy Bly looked smug. "Hunting always makes me hungry. So I've been harvesting."

"Harvesting what?"

Billy Bly's sharp yellow teeth glinted when he

smiled. "Don't worry. A hen's egg here, a water beetle there. Nothing anyone hereabouts would grudge me. I came to see why you called me."

"But I didn't." Frederick rubbed his eyes. He felt slow and a bit stupid. Maybe he had been closer to sleep than he'd thought.

"Why did you call me last night? His nibs interrupted you and cast the spell himself. But I'm not deaf. I heard you calling me."

"Oh, that." With Billy Bly lounging before him, Frederick felt silly about ever having thought the brownie was nothing but a dream. He didn't want to show what a baby he'd been about missing Billy Bly, so he chose his words with care. "I wanted to know more about the curse. I suppose it doesn't matter now, since Lord Schofield banished the thing."

At the mere mention of the curse, Billy Bly shivered.

"Tell me," Frederick went on, "why did you answer? Many times I've wished just to know you were around the place. What I wanted made no difference. Why answer my call now?"

"For the sake of time past and time to come," Billy Bly replied.

That sounded to Frederick like something Lord Schofield would say. "What does that mean?"

"Time past, because I've always liked you. Time to

come, because the day draws nigh I can't answer you at all. I won't hear you, and you won't hear me." Billy Bly looked grim. "Nothing mortal lasts."

"Wait." Frederick thought it over carefully. Mortal meant something that could die. "Are you telling me that you're dying?"

"No." Billy Bly held up his hand to cut off Frederick's next question before he asked it. "Now don't ask me if *you're* dying, for so far as I know, you aren't. No faster than any mortal creature, I promise you."

"Do you know the future?" Frederick demanded.

"I have no way to see your end or mine. But sometimes I can see beginnings." Billy Bly must have read Frederick's confusion in his expression. Patiently, he started over. "I came to say good-bye. Our parting is near. The new child calls me."

"The child Lady Schofield is carrying?" Frederick scowled. "How can that be? That child isn't even born yet."

"There are more spells on this house than the one Sir Hilary Bedrick cast. Magic runs in the Schofield family. Many a wizard has lived here before this one. They cast spells of protection. One of those spells has me in its power. If the owner's first child is born in this house, any brownie living here must serve that child and no other from the moment of its birth."

"You are already under the spell? Servant to a baby?

Before the child is even born?" The unfairness of it nearly took Frederick's breath away.

Billy Bly looked sad. "Aye, lad. More friend than servant, as I hope I have been to you. But the matter is settled."

Frederick could hardly speak, he was so angry. "Can't we break the spell?"

"A friendly thought, but no. This spell is too strong." Billy Bly looked more closely at Frederick. "Here, lad. Don't look so brokenhearted. I'm not bound to the child forever. Some of us serve until we are freed by gratitude. Some of us serve until we are given clothes. For me, I never serve more than one at a time, and I never serve more than seven years. Seven years and not one moment longer."

Frederick thought the lump in his throat might choke him. With all his heart, he wished he were dreaming. But he wasn't dreaming. Billy Bly had only come to say good-bye. "Will I ever see you again?"

"Never." Billy Bly's voice was full of regret. "Time runs swiftly, especially for a mortal like you. It would have been finished soon enough between us without this child's arrival."

"If I hadn't come here, you wouldn't have to do it." Frederick forced the words out. "This is all my fault."

"Never say that. Never even think it." Billy Bly tapped his chest. "It was my own doing to flit along with you so blithely. I didn't notice the spells laid upon this place until it was too late."

"I wish I'd never come here. I wish I'd never heard of Lord Schofield." Frederick broke off, gulping back the feelings that threatened to overtake him.

"Next you will say you wish you'd never left that orphanage, and we both know you don't mean that. I don't blame you. Not for anything." More gently, Billy Bly added, "If it is any comfort, know I chose you freely. No spells required. I chose well when I chose you. No regrets, young Frederick. If I could, I would choose you again."

Between one heartbeat and the next, Billy Bly vanished. The dressing room was as empty as the feeling in Frederick's stomach. For a moment, Frederick simply stared into the emptiness. Then he put out the candle. Eyes shut tight against the sight of the empty room, he curled back up in his blanket and lay silent as the last of the darkness yielded slowly to dawn.

Frederick did not let himself make a single sound. He certainly did not cry. What good would crying do? What good was anything?

⚜

When Frederick next opened his eyes, it was to the gloom of late afternoon. Even though it was scarcely tea time, the late October day was already yielding to dusk.

Frederick washed his face and tidied himself. It was odd that neither Lord Schofield nor Piers had needed him all day. He wondered if he really had been sacked. Were they just waiting for him to wake up to throw him out of the house? That didn't seem too likely.

When Frederick came cautiously out of the dressing room and down the back stairs, the whole house seemed oddly silent. Silent, that is, until he stepped into the kitchen, where every servant in the household seemed to have gathered, all of them shouting.

Frederick stepped up to the nearest cluster of servants, all housemaids. "What's happened?"

Pink with excitement, Rose turned to him, tumbling her words out so he scarcely understood her. "It's her ladyship! Her labor pains began two hours ago. Nearly a week earlier than I'd wagered, too. That's me sixpence poorer. His lordship has sent Foster and the curricle to London. He's to fetch the man-midwife. Just in case he doesn't come in time, Mrs. Kimball has sent one of the grooms to the village to fetch our midwife."

Frederick puzzled through the flurry of words too slowly to suit Rose. With a flash of impatience, she snapped, "The child is on the way. Lady Schofield's labor has begun."

"Oh, is that all?" Frederick didn't try to hide his resentment of the child as he looked from Rose to the chaos going on around them in the kitchen. "I thought perhaps a war had broken out."

"So it has, in a way." Mrs. Dutton loomed over them both. "It's a battle her ladyship is in now. You are no use underfoot here, Frederick, so off with you. Rose, if you can't think of anything better to do than gossip, find some work and do it. Or I'll find work for you."

Gratefully, Frederick escaped back upstairs to the dressing room. He still felt strange. Not just sad over his loss of Billy Bly. It was something more than that. Restlessness filled him. He tried to take Mrs. Dutton's advice and find some work to do. There were always boots to polish.

But try as he would, Frederick could not settle to polishing boots. His restlessness would not leave him. At last, although he knew he should keep on with his rags and polish, he cleaned his hands and ventured out again. He went up the back stairs instead of down. This time, he knew he was headed somewhere he had no business to go, the nursery.

With everyone else busy downstairs, the top floor of Skeynes was eerily silent. He heard the wind outside rattling at the windows, as if it was trying the latches over and over. As he moved down the corridor toward the nursery, every floorboard had a different creaky note underfoot to betray his steps.

The nursery door was open. Frederick stood on the threshold, just looking, for a long time.

Every windowpane shone, and the fresh white paint on the walls seemed to gleam. Braided rugs softened the polished wooden floorboards. Every stick of furniture was dusted. Every scrap of fabric was clean and pressed. A small fire smoldered into embers in the fireplace; all the warmth there was to keep the autumn chill at bay.

Frederick crossed the threshold and walked boldly around the room, touching this and that. He straightened up a rag doll slumped crookedly on a shelf. He set the rocking horse to rocking with a touch of his hand. He studied his reflection in the looking glass hung above the mantelpiece. He stood there, quite empty-handed. The child wasn't born yet, and already this whole room belonged to it. Not even Frederick's clothing truly belonged to him.

When the moment came, the child would be Billy Bly's master, blessed just to have parents. One day, if the child was a boy, the whole house and all its lands would belong to him. Every servant in the place would be his to command. And not just in this place. How many houses would the child inherit? How many servants would he have to do his bidding?

This child would be rich by any measure the world used. Why did the child have to have Billy Bly too? Billy Bly was all Frederick had ever had.

The embers on the hearth were dying. The room grew chill. Half out of habit, half to stop himself thinking, Frederick made up the fire afresh. When the flames were leaping merrily again, Frederick rested in the warmth, cross-legged on the hearth rug. He knew he should leave. He had no business in the nursery, no excuse to offer for his presence.

The colors of the fire held Frederick spellbound. More than the flames, he loved the shift and play of the burning embers. Inside every glowing coal, he could see the black heart of the fire. Blackness only made the colors lovelier. There would be no brightness without the dark, he thought.

With pure force of will, Frederick made himself rise above his feelings. So what if the child would never know his own luck? Weren't there plenty of children left back in the orphanage who would say the same of Frederick?

Perhaps Frederick had been born lucky too, and just didn't understand his own good fortune. All along, Frederick had believed he understood how lucky he was to have Billy Bly. Now he knew what it meant to have Billy Bly for a friend. Only now, when it was lost to him, did he truly value what a treasure he had possessed.

But Frederick hadn't truly lost Billy Bly yet. The spell did not take hold until the child was born. Perhaps it wouldn't be born. There had been trouble before. Perhaps Lady Schofield would lose this baby too.

That was an evil thought. With a shudder, Frederick banished it. He wished Lady Schofield no harm. Let her have her stupid baby. Let the baby have Billy Bly. Frederick would do without. He had done without a family all his life. He could do without Billy Bly.

Frederick rose and took a last look around. There was no trace he had ever been in the nursery. With a bit of good luck, there would soon be as much loud uproar in this room as there had been in the kitchen, a happy uproar of welcome for the infant. Let the luck be good. Let the baby be born safe and sound.

With some effort but with all his heart, Frederick wished good fortune to the child. A bit of happy uproar would be just what the old place needed, Frederick told himself, a bit of happy uproar and Billy Bly taking care of Skeynes and its new heir.

Wishing peels no onions, Frederick reminded himself, nor did it clean the boots. With an ear cocked for domestic uproar, he headed for Lord Schofield's dressing room. Even from the back stairs, he could hear the cries and shouted orders from Lady Schofield's bedchamber. Wincing in sympathy, he let himself into his refuge. Lord Schofield's second-best boots needed to be cleaned and polished. With hands that shook only a little, he selected the tools he needed and set to work.

Before Frederick was satisfied with the sheen on the first boot, the door to Lord Schofield's bedchamber slammed open. Lord Schofield, about as lively as a sack of coal, was hauled in, slung between Piers and Mr. Kimball. They put him on the bed, where he lay as if stunned. Frederick dropped the boot and the brush and sprang to help. "What's wrong with him?"

Lord Schofield was so pale he was nearly gray, his mouth a pinched line of pain. He was breathing hard, but made not a sound.

"Labor pains," Piers replied as Mr. Kimball left them alone with the wizard. "It's her ladyship. The worst of her travail has begun."

"What are you talking about?" Frederick looked up from pulling Lord Schofield's boots off. "Men don't have labor pains."

Groaning, Lord Schofield rolled away from Frederick the moment the second boot was free. The groans were indistinct, but Frederick thought he made out the word *Rats!*

"This one does." With difficulty, Piers removed first one of his employer's arms and then the other from the sleeves of his tight-fitting coat. "What he feels, she does. What she feels, he does. It all comes through the wedding ring she wears—he focused his magic in it."

"Traitor!" Lord Schofield failed to punch Piers in the nose, but only just. "That's a secret!"

"No one ever keeps a secret from his valet, nor from his assistant valet either." Piers had to sit upon Lord Schofield to get his waistcoat off. "Now, give over, my lord, do."

"Traitor!"

"Do calm yourself, sir." Piers was still calm, but his struggles to subdue Lord Schofield made him sound a little out of breath. "It's only Frederick and me here. You know you can trust us."

"Rats!" Lord Schofield roared. *"Rats!"*

Had the wizard gone mad? With all his heart, Frederick wished himself miles away. "Should I fetch a physician?"

"Rats," Lord Schofield growled, but as he was now facedown and chewing his pillow, Piers was able to release his grip upon the wizard and step away from the bed.

"No point. There's nothing any physician can do." Piers looked grim. "It was much like this when Lady Schofield lost the first child. He won't be in his right wits until it's all over."

From Piers's set expression, Frederick knew it was no time to ask questions. He and Piers made Lord Schofield as comfortable as they could.

Brandy helped. Once he had been made to stop biting the pillows, Lord Schofield calmed enough to sip from the glass Frederick held for him and say, "There are rats in Lady Schofield's bedchamber."

Piers drew back horrified. "My lord, that cannot be."

Lord Schofield glared at him. "I know that, Piers. No fleas, no rats, no mice, no bats. I cast the spell myself. It protects the whole estate. But with my own ears, I heard it. Rats in the walls of Lady Schofield's bedchamber. A rat—or something very like one." Lord Schofield took another sip. "A large rat. A tremendous—oh, devil take it, here it comes again—"

Lord Schofield doubled up, writhing. While Piers took the glass away and mopped at the brandy that had spilled on the bedclothes, Frederick caught Lord Schofield's hand. His grip made Frederick worry that Lord Schofield might twist his fingers clear off without even knowing what he did.

In five minutes, the worst of that wave of pain had passed. Lord Schofield sank back into his pillows again, panting and mumbling. Frederick rubbed sensation back into his numbed fingers.

Piers helped himself to the last sip of brandy. "The first time he went into labor, it was just groans and whimpers. Not a word about rats."

"I'll whimper you," Lord Schofield wheezed.

From his days at the orphanage, Frederick was well acquainted with rats and their ways. "Begging your pardon, my lord, there was something in the chimneys, as you know very well, but it wasn't rats."

"I'm not senile, Frederick. I banished that thing in

the chimney. I remember doing so. But there are rats in the chimney now. Rats in Kate's chamber." Lord Schofield seemed to be addressing someone else, someone Frederick couldn't see. "Rats in the walls. Fetch out that rat so I can banish it. I'd fetch it myself if I could only sit up." The pangs returned with greater force than before, and Lord Schofield's words were reduced to moans.

"You stay with him. I will see what there is to be done," Frederick told Piers. "If he takes a notion to try to get out of bed, I'm not big enough to stop him."

"Excellent idea," said Piers. "I'm not fond of rats. Even very small ones disgust me."

"It's not a rat." Frederick caught himself. There was no point in wasting time talking to Piers. "Oh, never mind. I'll be back as soon as I can."

IN WHICH FREDERICK
DEMONSTRATES HIS SKILL

The moment he arrived at the door to Lady Schofield's bedchamber, Frederick gave up his first plan,
which was to tap at the walls and listen for sounds that
should not be there. There was no chance of hearing a
rat, no matter how large, because the place was so full
of noise. Everywhere he looked, there were maids in a
hurry. They carried basins of boiling water, bundles of
clean linen, and cups of hot tea. He could hear moans
and cries of pain from Lady Schofield, but they were
all but drowned out by crisp orders, well-meant advice,
and excited chatter from all and sundry.

Rather than tapping on the walls, Frederick found
himself under Mrs. Dutton's direct supervision as she
set him raking ashes and making up the fire.

"That's the lad," said Mrs. Dutton. "Nancy, stir
your stumps. Go ask if the midwife has come yet."

"I'll go." Frederick headed toward the door with only a bucket of ashes to dispose of downstairs.

"Those can wait," Mrs. Dutton said, taking the bucket from him as she handed him a basket of soiled sheets. "Take these down to the laundry."

From the wall above the fireplace came a dull thud.

"What on earth?" Mrs. Dutton glared first at the wall and then at Frederick. "Not even Lord Schofield would cast a spell at a time like this. Would he?"

Before Frederick could answer, the thump came again, less distinctly, from the corridor outside. Still clutching the basket of sheets, Frederick followed the thump. He caught up with it down the hall, then lost it. He hesitated outside Lord Schofield's bedchamber.

"Rat!" From within, Lord Schofield shouted, "What did I tell you!"

Frederick entered expecting to see a rat the size of a sheep. Instead, he found Lord Schofield sitting up in bed. Piers, with the fireplace poker in his hand, was standing as close to the fire as he dared, trying to see up into the chimney. There was no rat whatsoever.

"It was a snake. I saw it!" Eyes wild, Piers waved the poker to show Frederick where it had gone.

"Come away from the fire," said Frederick. "You'll burn yourself."

"You didn't see it!" Piers turned from Frederick back

to the fireplace. "A snake as big around as my arm."

From up the flue came a noise like a mattress splitting open. There was an ear-piercing squeal, a shower of soot, and Billy Bly fell out onto the hearth rug, wrestling something that looked like a black snake.

"Billy Bly!" Frederick dropped the basket of soiled sheets.

"There it is!" Piers swung the poker with enthusiasm. The fire irons fell over with a clatter. Ashes scattered. Sparks flew. A china dish fell off the mantelpiece and shattered.

"Watch it!" Billy Bly snarled. "Hit me with that thing again and I'll wrap it around your head."

"Then get out of the way!" Piers took another wild swing, then added, "Thought you were part of it. Sorry."

The black snake coiled around Piers's right leg and he fell over, swearing. The space before the hearth was full of something black. Something writhing. It was huge.

Frederick reached into the basket he had just dropped, seized a handful of a soiled linen sheet, and dived into the tangle. When he touched the black thing, his hand tingled. He clenched his jaw and made himself take a firm grip, even though the tingle made his elbow twinge and his wrist ache.

Using the very first knot Vardle had ever taught

him, Frederick tied the corner of the linen sheet to the creature. Tying a bowline knot with a rope was easy. Tying it with a twisted sheet was hard. Frederick panted and pulled until the black snake was held fast by the straining fabric.

"Good lad!" Billy Bly grunted. "We'll hold it whilst you bind it."

The black thing struggled silently, trying to work its way back to the safety of the flue, but Frederick's knot held.

As he tied the other end of the sheet to one of the bedposts, Frederick spared a moment to wonder who held whom faster, Billy Bly and Piers or the black thing. "There now. Let go and his lordship can set to work banishing it."

But Lord Schofield was doubled up again, roaring with pain.

"Oh, you're useless," Frederick said as he leaped back into the tangle to help Piers free his leg from the black thing.

Beside them, Billy Bly clung stubbornly to the black thing. Where his gnarled hands clutched, the soot had rubbed away. Beneath, the creature was shiny, like woven silk. It was the color of twilight, and the more Frederick looked at it, the less certain he was of what he saw. To his eyes, it was a snake, a rope, a thick silken cord. But to his arms, it pulled like a cart horse. Only the knotted sheet kept it in the room. Even so, it pulled so hard the bed was slowly creeping closer to the fireplace.

"Steady on, lads," said Billy Bly. "Heave ho."

"I'm with you," Frederick cried. "Heave ho!"

"My leg!" Groaning and moaning, Piers made almost as much noise as Lord Schofield did. "You'll have it out of the socket!"

"Stop squirming." Frederick worked to help Billy Bly pull the thing off Piers. The black thing seemed to bulge and flex in his grip as if there were muscles working beneath that shadowy surface.

"Get it off me!" Piers shouted.

Frederick kept tugging despite the bulging in the creature. The shadowy surface changed as he watched. No longer shiny, it looked and felt bristly, but not with the familiar bristly roughness of an ordinary rope. It felt like hair, long wet hair that tangled around Frederick's fingers and pinched his flesh. Frederick wanted to drop the rope and wipe his hands on his breeches until both the tingling and the tangling were gone, but instead he held on.

"Take this." Billy Bly poked Frederick in the ribs. He had left the struggle so stealthily that Frederick had not noticed he was gone until he had returned. Billy Bly was holding a bundle of white cloth under one arm as he used his free hand to get Frederick's attention. "I can't hold it much longer, even with the cloth wrapped around it. Cold steel burns me."

Frederick took a better look and saw Billy Bly was offering him one of Lord Schofield's straight razors wrapped up in a clean cravat. "What's that for? We don't have time for a shave just now."

"Take it." Billy Bly poked Frederick harder. "It's made of steel."

At last, Frederick thought he understood. "Wait—you mean steel hurts it?"

"Cold steel *burns*." Billy Bly stood clear as Frederick took the razor carefully by its ivory grip. Frederick slid the blade carefully between the black thing and the fabric of Piers's breeches.

"What are you doing?" Piers goggled at him. "Easy with that thing. You'll have my leg off!"

"Isn't this thing going to squeeze your leg off anyway?" Frederick said. "Hold still."

"Thanks," said Piers in a very small voice. "I think I will."

At the first touch of the steel razor, the black thing shuddered and went limp. Piers eased away from the blade.

"Does it hate steel that much?" Frederick wondered.

Billy Bly growled, "Don't be tricked."

Warned and watchful, Frederick kept his grip firm

on both the black thing and the steel razor. Swearing softly, Piers freed himself and stood between the bed and the fireplace, rubbing his leg. On the bed, Lord Schofield was still and silent, mute and sweating with pain. Frederick could detect no motion in the piece of the black thing he held. For a moment he was tempted to try shaving the long hairs so they wouldn't tickle his hand so unpleasantly.

As the rest of its bulk slithered from flue to fireplace, the other end of the black thing brought a choking drift of smoke into the room, or Frederick would never have turned his head and seen it slip into the room. Billy Bly growled deep in his chest. "Beware, lad."

The end of the black thing that Frederick had tied to the bed still looked rough and hairy. But the other end, the end that had just slid through the fire unharmed, was smooth and shiny. The shiny end of the rope was groping its way blindly toward the knot in the dirty sheet that Frederick had tied around its tail.

To Frederick, the thing looked like a snake, but a snake with no eyes, no features, no head at all, only a gleaming shell over the mindless strength within.

Frederick had to put the razor away to do it, but he hauled out another soiled sheet and tied the headless snake's gleaming shell to the hairy tail with the second knot he'd ever learned, the one that made a rope shorter without cutting it. As he hauled on the sheet to tighten his knot, the black thing went limp again.

Frederick and Piers exchanged a long look, shuddering with relief. Frederick felt as if his heart was ready to jump out of his chest. Piers looked as if he might faint.

"Hold fast, Frederick." Without warning, Billy Bly's whole attitude changed from wariness to wild cheer. He sprang away from the tangled mess to the dressing room door. "Good-bye, lad. Fare thee well." For a moment he stood poised as if listening to music no one else could hear, then he turned back to Frederick. "I wish we had been granted our full seven years."

"No, wait—" Frederick began.

"Time has come!" Billy Bly called out, "The child is here!" Between one hard-thumping beat of Frederick's heart and the next, Billy Bly had vanished.

"No!" Set to follow Billy Bly, Frederick pulled his hands free of the sheets. At once, he discovered his mistake.

The black thing's headless coils ripped free of the knotted sheets the moment he released his grip. Quick as thought, the scaly end of the thing wrapped around Lord Schofield's throat. Only Piers's desperate grip on the thing kept it from snapping the wizard's neck. Lord Schofield made a noise that would have been a scream if he'd had any breath for it.

Piers swore.

Frederick, struggling beside Piers, knew exactly how he felt.

So the child was here, was it? That was enough to pull Billy Bly away, to leave Frederick and Piers alone with this monster? Hot resentment flooded Frederick as he fumbled for the razor. What more did Frederick need from Billy Bly? With a razor in his hand, he was far from harmless. Frederick had more than a razor; he had the knowledge it took to use it well.

Determination brought icy calm. "Mind your fingers, Piers." Frederick's anger made him quick and his fear made him careful. With a deft flick of the wrist, he slid the steel blade between Piers's hands and pulled downward. Deftly, Frederick cut Lord Schofield free. The wizard fell back against his pile of pillows, hands to his bruised throat. No help from that quarter.

With great care, Frederick used the blade, slice upon slice, to carve the thing. The creature had no head, no mouth, no means to scream. Yet, furious, it screamed. Frederick felt it in his hands. The hairy tail caught Frederick a stinging blow on the forehead as he worked to free Lord Schofield. Another struck his nose. Frederick tasted blood.

The creature was oozing something black and sticky as slices of it came away. The pieces that fell on the floor wriggled toward each other, as if hoping to reunite. Piers sprang away and gathered bits up before they could touch. He tossed one in the chamber pot, one in Lord Schofield's top hat, one in each of the boots discarded on the floor. In isolation, the bits went still. Frederick didn't trust that stillness. Hands covered in ooze, he kept on cutting, carving, slicing, chopping.

By the time he had the creature reduced to bits small enough to fit in a pocket, Frederick was out of breath. "This razor is done for. The edge will never be the same."

"Never mind." Piers was shoulder to shoulder with him, equally soiled and sticky. "It died honorably. Still six left. Never saw a closer shave, lad. Well done."

Lord Schofield sat up in bed. "Kate's done it!" he croaked. "The child is here!" With a bound, he left the bed to leap to his feet. At once his knees buckled, and he fell to the floor swearing. "Give me your hand, Piers. I must go congratulate Kate. What a woman. She's turned the trick."

"Congratulate Frederick first," Piers retorted, levering Lord Schofield to his feet. "He saved your life."

"Yes, by God, he did! Although the task isn't finished until these, these . . ." Lord Schofield searched for the correct word and snapped his fingers when he found it. "These cutlets have been disposed of. But thank you, Frederick. I'm grateful to you. The moment I have a bit of peace and quiet, I'll dispose of this disgusting debris properly. No time now, though. Do hurry, Piers!"

Piers hauled Lord Schofield away. Frederick found himself alone in Lord Schofield's bedchamber. Everywhere he looked was soot and ooze and soiled linen. His nose had stopped bleeding, but the bruise on his forehead grew more painful by the moment.

Frederick washed the black stuff off the ruined razor. Ruined it might be, but it deserved respect, so he buffed it dry out of habit, oiled it, and put it carefully away. The simple ritual helped him calm down. Little by little, his heartbeat came back to normal.

Doggedly he set about tidying the worst of the mess. Frederick's head was aching, his eyes burning with tiredness. By the time he was finished, the word was out, from the cellars to the attic rooms of Skeynes. Lord and Lady Schofield were proud parents of an heir, a son. The child was healthy, strong, and loud. So loud, indeed, that in the vicinity of Lady Schofield's bedchamber voices had to shout to be heard over the infant's wails.

The whole house was a hubbub of relief and joy. Frederick scrubbed his hands and took himself down to the servants' hall. Bess was there before him. She beamed at him as he joined her. "Isn't it wonderful?"

Mrs. Dutton was serving out bread and milk in bowls to anyone who asked for it nicely. Frederick looked around the kitchen. "Where's Grant?"

"Gone to fetch the champagne from the wine cellar," Mrs. Dutton answered. "We'll not see him again in a hurry, nor Mr. Kimball neither."

"Have you seen the baby? He's ever so tiny, for all he's so loud," Bess continued.

Frederick made it a point to spoon up bread and milk so that, instead of joining Bess in her raptures over the new heir, he had his mouth too full to do more than smile at her and nod. He didn't want to talk about how wonderful the new child was going to be. Miserable brat.

Bess said, "Did you know there's blood on your shirt? Frederick, what have you done to your head? It looks like you're trying to grow a horn. Does it hurt? Mrs. Dutton, may we have something for Frederick's head?"

Mrs. Dutton chuckled, "Bless you, have what you please. It will be a holiday around here for days. What about a nice slice of plum cake? Do either of you fancy that?"

Mrs. Dutton took care of the bump on Frederick's forehead. Then Bess and Frederick ate as much plum cake as they could hold. When at last he rose from the table, Frederick was feeling much better. Still, the thought of those pieces of the black thing troubled him. Lord Schofield had given orders to leave them until he could dispose of them properly. But the wizard was likely to be distracted by the arrival of his son. What if two of those pieces managed to wriggle back together?

Back upstairs, Frederick found the door to the bed-chamber locked. He put his ear to the door panel and heard nothing. He knocked.

After a moment, Lord Schofield opened the door. "Ah. Frederick. You aren't needed just now."

Frederick could not see beyond Lord Schofield's bulk, but he had the sense there was someone else in the room within. It made him curious. "I can help."

"You have helped." Lord Schofield smiled down at Frederick. "You have helped tremendously. But just now, I am rather busy. Go away."

"I sleep in the dressing room," Frederick reminded him. "With this door locked, I can't go to bed."

"Is it that late?" Lord Schofield looked surprised. "So it is. Well, it's a big house. Find somewhere else to sleep. Good night." With that, the wizard closed and locked the door.

Typical. Frederick glared at the door. Not so very long ago, he had saved Lord Schofield from death by strangulation. The wizard had said he was grateful, but how did he show it? Save a man's life and he locked your bed away.

When he put his ear to the door again, Frederick heard Lord Schofield intoning something. As usual, Frederick could not make out any words, but just once he thought he heard Billy Bly's deep voice.

To his horror, Frederick felt his eyes sting with tears at the sound. *Crying,* that would never do. He wiped his nose on his sleeve and squared his shoulders. Leave tears to babies, he told himself. Assistant valets don't cry.

Frederick listened at the door a long time, but the deep note did not recur. At last he gave up and went downstairs to sleep by the kitchen fire. The loudest of the reveling in the servants' hall had worn itself out, so the place was almost quiet. Frederick told himself it was no worse than he'd had it at the orphanage, sleeping in the kitchen. The floor was cleaner. Even banked for the night, the fire was warmer.

There was even a saucer of cream left beside the hearth, Grant's offering to Billy Bly. Frederick drank the cream himself, curled up beside the fire, and slept.

IN WHICH FREDERICK
TIDIES UP

Almost before he knew he'd been asleep, Frederick woke to the smell of fresh bread. He scrambled out of the cook's way.

"Rough night?" Grant asked. "There's a lot of that about this morning."

Frederick couldn't think of anything to say to that. He leaned against the wall while he yawned and stretched himself awake.

"Half the household stayed up drinking themselves stupid to celebrate the new heir." Grant's tone made his low opinion of less hardy drinkers plain. "They'll be sorry when they finally wake up and find they still have all their work left to do and only part of the day to do it in."

"Not guilty," said Frederick. "Never touched a drop."

"Then why were you sleeping on the floor?" The cook sliced the end of a loaf of bread in two, buttered both halves an inch thick, and pushed one piece over to Frederick. "Hang about. There's a bit of bacon coming."

"Locked out." Frederick licked his fingers and waited for the bacon. When it came, still sizzling from the fire, he ate his share so fast he burned his tongue. He sucked in air and fanned his mouth. "Thank you," he mumbled, when he was able to speak again.

"Oh, greedy." Grant seemed to take Frederick's enthusiasm as a great compliment. "No more for you, lad."

Frederick wiped his mouth and brushed the last bread crumbs to the floor. "Good, that. Well worth the pain."

"Praise indeed," said Grant. "Will his lordship want his breakfast any time this morning, do you think? Or will he stay in bed the whole day and sleep it off?"

Frederick remembered that he was angry with the whole world, most particularly with Lord Schofield. It would suit him fine if the ungrateful toad missed breakfast for a week. Still, he didn't want Grant to get in trouble. "I'll go see if he's likely to stir any time this year."

"Thanks." Grant returned to his work, readying breakfast for the entire household.

By the halfhearted light of the rainy autumn morning, Frederick climbed the back stairs, marveling at how silent the house was. After the noise of the night before, the place seemed cold and lonely. The sense of warmth and belonging he had known in the months he'd lived in the house was gone. Had it all been Billy Bly's influence on him? Had he ever truly felt at home at Skeynes?

The door to Lord Schofield's bedchamber stood open. The wizard was nowhere to be seen. From the state of the wash basin and the wardrobe, Frederick guessed he had gone to see his wife and child the moment he was washed and dressed.

Marveling, Frederick gazed around the bedchamber. Scarcely a trace remained of the battle they had fought here the day before. Nothing betrayed the magical work Lord Schofield had performed in the night. Had Billy Bly been at work here? Frederick looked around more closely.

Except for the unmade bed and his lordship's usual morning disorder, everything was where it belonged. Most of it was clean, so clean Frederick had to pinch himself to believe his eyes. Only his lordship's top hat, kicked into a corner, lingered to hint at yesterday's struggle.

Frederick inspected the top hat as he brushed it clean. Restoring the glossy black gleam to the exterior was easy enough. Careful examination of the inside of the hat revealed lingering traces of the sticky black stuff. Frederick got out the powdered chalk used to clean the tops of Lord Schofield's hunting boots and rubbed it into the stains. When the chalk had soaked up as much of the stain as possible, he brushed the powder out and started again with a fresh handful.

As he worked, Frederick hummed a little tune, oddly content with a task that asked nothing of him but patience and persistence. Persistence, it occurred to Frederick, was a particular strength of his. It made him feel good to work stubbornly away, knowing he was going to triumph eventually. Sitting there, saving the top hat from the stain, the work gave him a sense of peace. All might not be right with the world, but just for that moment, all was right with Frederick.

After the top hat, there were the second-best riding boots, forgotten in all the excitement, still to be polished. Frederick worked his way through the bedchamber and dressing room, cleaning what was already gleamingly clean, tidying what was already tidy. Half the morning had slipped away before Frederick noticed.

The work was easy because, except for a thimbleful of stain in the top hat, none of his efforts were needed. Frederick pondered that thought. Perhaps none of his work ever had been needed. Perhaps it was time, very likely it was past time, that he moved on. Found a better situation. Somewhere his skills would be truly appreciated.

Frederick was still considering that idea when the door flew open. Lord Schofield sprang into the room. "Frederick! I want boots! Bring me my driving coat, my hat—oh, and gloves. But boots first! Boots above all! First, last, and always, I must have boots."

Frederick did not need a single word of these orders to gauge his master's temper. The speed and ease with which Lord Schofield moved made all plain. Despite his shouting, he was in a wonderful humor.

"Can you believe it? That dunce of a man-midwife has found his way here at last. Finally thought to read the letter I sent when I summoned him, I suppose."

"The child was born early," Frederick reminded him. "He wouldn't have expected to hear from you for another week."

"Not *those* boots. Don't toy with me, lad. Your senses are keen. Your instincts about the soot in the chimney prove it."

Before Frederick could thank him for the compliment, Lord Schofield was chattering on. "Keener wits than Pickering's, and don't think for an instant I won't give him a wigging for missing a warning sign plain even to my assistant valet. Now, given the sharpness of your eyes and wits, how can it have escaped your attention that it is raining? I don't fancy ruining my best pair of boots to help that dozy wretch avoid the rain."

Frederick began to help Lord Schofield put on the second-best boots, the ones he'd just finished polishing.

Without a word of thanks, Lord Schofield went right on talking. "Just as well Kate finished the job with the midwife from the village. Now the man-midwife is finally here, I find I don't care for the look of him above half. Chances are he would have fallen asleep in the middle of the proceedings, the—" Lord Schofield caught himself and all too obviously changed his mind about what he was going to say. "The lazy creature."

"My lord!" In his surprise, Frederick dropped the boot he was holding. "*Lazy creature?* Your language is usually far stronger than that."

"In the past, I have used strong language. I admit it. When provoked," Lord Schofield added. "But that's all changed. As the father of a son, I must set an example. From today, I shall moderate my language. As of this morning, I am a reformed character."

"Very good, my lord." Frederick went back to helping with the boots, glad he was doubled over so his face was hidden. It would never do to let Lord Schofield see his expression. If he didn't laugh in the wizard's face, Frederick would consider it a lucky escape.

"The sooner we're rid of the man-midwife the better. I have business in Stroud. That is the location of his next delivery, so he claims."

Frederick finished with the boots and straightened up. "That's lucky."

"Isn't it just?" Lord Schofield arched an eyebrow. "I wonder how happy his new employers will be to have him on their doorstep prematurely. Probably eats his clients out of house and home." As he inspected himself in the looking glass, Lord Schofield fell silent. He seemed fascinated, first by his own reflection, then by his hat. At length, he turned and held the top hat out to Frederick. "Frederick. What have you done to this hat?"

"Cleaned it, sir." Frederick turned to look for the second-best top hat. "You won't want to ruin that in the rain either, will you? I'll fetch another."

"You cleaned it?" Even as he glared at Frederick, Lord Schofield had turned the hat over and was sniffing at the silk lining. "The devil you say. Last night I cleaned it of the residue myself, and it didn't smell like this then. What did you use?"

Frederick decided that if a good clean top hat wasn't to Lord Schofield's taste, there was no point in wasting any effort trying to please him. Better to give his notice and get it over with. "Powdered chalk, my lord. Same as I use on your boot tops."

"Powdered *chalk*?" Lord Schofield held the top hat up to the light and tapped at the crown. "Unusual. Oatmeal, I would have guessed. Best steel-cut Scottish oats."

"I would have had to go down to the kitchens for that," Frederick replied. "The chalk was already here."

"Powdered chalk and what else?" Lord Schofield demanded. "Lavender water?"

Frederick shook his head.

"Salzburg vitriol? Hungary water?" Lord Schofield guessed. "Plum blossom?"

Frederick couldn't help laughing a little. "At this time of year, sir? Nothing else. Just powdered chalk."

"Nonsense. There's something else. What exactly did you do with the powdered chalk?"

"I just rubbed it into the stains, sir."

"And?" Lord Schofield had glared at Frederick before, but now he scowled ferociously. "Be honest, now. What else did you do?"

Frederick thought it over for a long time before he shrugged and gave up. "Nothing. I hummed a bit. That's all. Honestly, my lord." He hummed a piece of the song, *peas and beans, corn and rye,* then remembered where he had heard it first—Billy Bly singing in the night—and stopped.

"You hummed a bit." Lord Schofield put the hat back on and regarded himself in the looking glass. He uttered a series of hooting grunts and gazed inquiringly at Frederick. "Is that it?"

"Is what it?" Frederick asked blankly.

"Is that the tune you were humming?"

That was meant to be humming? Wisely, Frederick did not speak his thoughts. "I suppose so. Why? Have I done something wrong?"

His resolve to reform apparently forgotten, Lord Schofield said a very bad word indeed. "I have been a blockhead. No, Frederick. You've done nothing wrong. But I know a spell when I find one under my nose. Or, perhaps I should say, just above it. You tell me you were humming while you cleaned this hat with powdered chalk. The traces of it will be with me until you take the spell off." Lord Schofield tossed the hat back to Frederick. "Take it off later, with a clean soft cloth and a dab of spirits of hartshorn. No humming, mind! For now, bring me my second-best top hat."

The best top hat fell from Frederick's hands. "But— But—I didn't *do* a spell. I didn't ground anything. I just cleaned that black stuff out of your hat."

"And precisely what *was* that black stuff?"

"Stuff from the curse." Frederick thought it over and added, falteringly, "Magic?"

"You see things in the fire." Lord Schofield was beaming at Frederick. "And I always thought there was more to that boot polishing of yours than met the eye."

"That was Billy Bly," Frederick reminded him.

"Part of it," Lord Schofield agreed. "The rest was you, Frederick. *You*. Same goes for the way you tie a neck cloth, or make a bed, or scrub a stain off the floor. You get yourself put into things properly, you'll never come out, even with spirits of hartshorn."

"Magic." Frederick thought it over, remembering the sense of peace that had filled him as he had worked away at the top hat. "You make it sound like grass stains."

"Far more amusing than grass stains." Lord Schofield caught himself. "No, I don't mean that. What I meant to say is, magic is dangerous! You must be on your guard at all times. Oh, fetch me the other hat, you sluggard! I meant to drive to the bookseller in Stroud for my own entertainment. But now I find my journey truly necessary. I am in need of an elementary Greek primer."

"A Greek primer, sir? Why?" As he fetched the second-best top hat from its box, Frederick went on. "You can read Greek easy as kiss my hand. Why go out in the rain to buy a book you don't need?"

"For you, young man, for you." Lord Schofield put on his driving coat, a garment so generously cut that it doubled his width. "The study of classical Greek will protect you from the worst of the perils you will face as a student of magic. It's important not to cast spells in your native tongue. In theory, the use of Greek provides a layer—insulation of a sort—between your intention and the power that you call on to execute your spell."

Frederick was not sure whether Lord Schofield was joking or giving him his first magic lesson. Just to make certain, as he handed over the top hat, he tested his employer with a question intended to make him roar with laughter. "I am to learn Greek?"

"Classical Greek." Far from laughing at Frederick, Lord Schofield seemed perfectly serious.

"I am to learn Greek?" Frederick stared up at him. "But who will teach me?"

"I will." Lord Schofield looked pleased with himself. "If you prove an apt student, when you are ready for more advanced instruction in magic, I shall arrange it."

"Wait." Frederick could not take it in. "I am to learn magic?"

"If you prove an apt student. I'll find you the right tutor myself. Pickering, perhaps. Serve him right for his overconfidence." Lord Schofield set his second-best top hat at just the right angle and turned for the door. "Be warned. I intend to order Kimball to engage a new assistant valet. Soon you must train someone else to black my boots and press my neck cloths. No pushing the task off on Piers. He's hopeless with neck cloths."

When Lord Schofield had gone, Frederick stood before the looking glass and said to his own thunderstruck reflection, "Blow me down."

Then, wondering if he was still asleep and dreaming it all, Frederick went to tell Mr. Grant that Lord Schofield had gone out.

Halfway down the back stairs, Frederick met Bess on her way up with a basket of clean linen.

"You look so strange. What's wrong?" Bess felt his forehead. "Are you ill?"

"No." It took Frederick a few tries to get started, but once the words began to come, they tumbled out until he'd told her everything.

Bess beamed at him. "So you're to learn magic?"

"I'll try." Frederick broke off, overwhelmed by the sheer size of the task before him.

"You'll do it." Bess seemed able to read his feelings in his face. "If he didn't believe you could do it, Lord Schofield would never waste a moment of his valuable time on you."

"*That's* true enough." Frederick stood up a little straighter.

"I'm so proud of you." Bess added, "Not surprised, mind. Fingers as deft as yours—it stands to reason there's magic in them somehow." She gave him a quick kiss on the cheek and brushed past him with her basket on her hip. "Now, if I don't get Mrs. Dutton these sheets, she'll box my ears for certain." With steps quick and light as a dancer, Bess was on her way.

Frederick just stood there until the last of Bess's footsteps faded into silence. If Bess thought he could do it, then he could. He already knew the housework magic required. He could learn to be a wizard.

Frederick collected himself and set off for the kitchen. He still had to tell Mr. Grant that today Lord Schofield would require no breakfast whatsoever.

IN WHICH FREDERICK TRAINS
HIS REPLACEMENT

By Yuletide, deep midwinter had closed in on Skeynes. The skies were cold iron. The roads were mud. Frederick had never been busier. When he was not practicing the most basic elements of magical spells, he was memorizing lists of Greek words set him by Lord Schofield. When he was not studying, he was in Lord Schofield's dressing room, teaching.

"Stand up straight." Frederick poked his student into position.

Bess's brother, Clarence, was the new assistant valet. He had come all the way from London by mail coach. It was a good thing Bess was around to keep an eye on him, for he was already homesick for the rest of his family in London.

Clarence's hands were still small, which meant he was good at detail work. Frederick showed him everything he knew about using a smoothing iron, and Clarence fairly soaked it up. He knew any dallying or familiarity would be reported to Bess immediately. So he spoke less than ever, but he worked hard and learned fast.

Frederick showed Clarence just how much starch to put in Lord Schofield's neck cloths. He taught him the trick of folding the fabric when pressing it. Clarence was at his very best polishing leather, but he was a keen student on other topics as well. He took to the work of an assistant valet—every duty but one: tying the cravat.

"Look, it's easy." Frederick smoothed the worst of the wrinkles out of the practice neck cloth they were using and stood in front of Clarence. "Stand up straight. Now, look at the ceiling."

At first Clarence stared patiently upward while Frederick wrapped his neck in fabric. But before the wrapping was complete, Clarence moved his head as if he were listening intently. "What was that?"

For a moment, Frederick stopped what he was doing to listen. There was nothing to hear, no sound that did not properly belong to the household. "What was what?"

"There it is again." Clarence was staring upward. "Don't you hear that?"

"Hear what?" Frederick seized the ends of the neck cloth and lifted them into position. "It's important to keep the fabric taut while you wrap the cravat. Stop that fidgeting."

"What *is* that?" Clarence craned his neck. Ignoring Frederick completely, he was staring all around the room, as if he expected an attack but did not yet know from which direction it would come. "What's that rustling?"

Frederick froze. There was no rustling that he could hear. But was there a familiar sense of peace and companionship? Frederick released Clarence's neck cloth and tried to soothe him. "Even a small house can make strange noises now and then. Wood dries out; stones settle. A big old place like this? Might be anything at all."

"I know about old houses. This isn't anything like that. It sounds like the wind in the trees." By now Clarence was looking ready to jump out the window at the next shadow he saw. "What *is* that?"

"Forget it." Frederick put the neck cloth aside and found a length of string. "Look, let me show you another way. You can learn to tie the knot in a bit of string first. We'll work up to using the neck cloth. As soon as I finish that Greek primer, Lord Schofield will send me to study with Mr. Pickering. I'm not going to be here forever to explain things, so mark me well. Here's the first thing you need to know about tying knots, in a cravat or anything else."

◡◡

In the deep midwinter, at the great house called Skeynes, day dimmed to evening. The big house glowed with simple comfort and careful housekeeping. In Lord Schofield's dressing room, there was warmth and light and work to do.

For Frederick, there was peace. He never saw Billy Bly anymore. He couldn't hear even the faintest note of his deep voice. Yet Frederick was certain Billy Bly was near. He took comfort from the knowledge. For the next seven years, the brownie would watch over the whole household at Skeynes, not just the infant heir.

There was serenity in that, to Frederick's way of thinking. Back in London, in the days of Billy Bly's banishment, when Frederick's senses had worked perfectly, there had been no Billy Bly in the house to watch over them. Better this way, Frederick promised himself. Far better.

When seven years had passed, what then? Frederick was already determined to learn as much magic as he could. If he was good enough at magic in seven years, perhaps he would be able to call Billy Bly by himself. Perhaps someday he would see the brownie again, not because he needed him. Frederick wanted to ask how Billy Bly had tailored the suit of livery to fit him, and to thank him for all he had done.

When Frederick dismissed Clarence for the day, he

added one last duty to the list. "Now and then, put down a dish of cream. Take care not to let it stay too long, for it will sour if it goes untouched. But every week or so, leave out a dish of cream."

"Why?" Clarence looked confused. "Does Lord Schofield keep a cat in his bedchamber now?"

"No cat," Frederick said. "Do it anyway. That's my advice to you. The freshest, best cream available."

ACCORDING TO BESS

Botheration the feeling you have when being bothered, especially by a younger brother.

Brownie a sort of hobgoblin. They look like fat little old men in brown or green clothing. Sometimes they help with housework at night. They claim to like a quiet life, but if they are around, it's seldom quiet for long.

Chivy to maneuver someone about. It's a bit like shooing hens.

Chop-logic one who reasons so cleverly, he begs for an argument.

Clack to chatter without saying much.

Curricle a light carriage drawn by two horses, usually the fastest in the stable.

Dozy half asleep, especially when you're supposed to be wide-awake.

Farthing the smallest coin minted, worth one-fourth of a penny.

Flux what wizards use to get things done. They claim it means the rate of flow of fluid, particles, or energy.

Hungary water	a distillation of herbs and blossoms, usually rosemary, orange flowers, and lavender. It smells good, and it does wonders for a headache.
Nibs	one way to refer to the boss, but only when he's not around to hear you.
Pie-faced	looking a bit stupid.
Salzburg vitriol	copper sulfate, some wizards call it.
Sauce	impertinence.
Scaff and raff	rascals, riff-raff, or rabble.
Soppiness	sentimentality or mushiness.
Spirits of hartshorn	something a bit like ammonia; wizards say this started out as a distillation made from shavings of antler or horn.
Still room	the room where food and drink is preserved and distilled for the entire household.
Strop	this can be either a fit of very bad temper or the strap a valet uses to sharpen a razor.
Washing blue	this is bluing, the stuff you put in to make laundry look whiter. Sometimes people use Salzburg vitriol, but I wouldn't.
Wigging	a good scolding, by which I mean a bad one.